BANCROFT'S BANCO

Center Point
Large Print

Also by Nelson Nye and available from Center Point Large Print:

The Leather Slapper
Wildcats of Tonto Basin
Deadly Companions
The Texas Gun
Smoke Talk
Wide Loop

BANCROFT'S BANCO

NELSON NYE

CENTER POINT LARGE PRINT
THORNDIKE, MAINE

This Center Point Large Print edition
is published in the year 2022 by arrangement with
Golden West Inc.

Originally published in the US by Ace Books.

The text of this Large Print edition is unabridged.
In other aspects, this book may vary
from the original edition.
Printed in the United States of America
on permanent paper sourced using
environmentally responsible foresting methods.
Set in 16-point Times New Roman type.

ISBN 978-1-63808-563-8 (hardcover)
ISBN 978-1-63808-567-6 (paperback)

The Library of Congress has cataloged this record
under Library of Congress Control Number: 2022944029

I

Linda Ybarra.

She had olive skin, the high cheekboned look which generations of blueblooded *castellanos* had bred into her, the eyes and mouth of a flamenco dancer and the pale golden hair of her Catalonian ancestors. These, while attractive . . . even to my New England notions exotic, did not add up to any breathtaking beauty. The nose was too aquiline, top stubbornly determined. She was breathtaking enough. She was near to becoming a damnable nuisance.

Yet . . . what could I say?

Talk is tinder. One ill chosen word and all I had worked for, everything I'd put into this, could go up the spout and down the drain, blown apart like black powder, like a spinning dust-devil roaring over these bottoms.

Even to think of it was frightening.

It had looked so damned good, so incredibly simple—really foolproof I'd thought when the notion first struck me. All those pieces of land changing hands on the whim of a storm, a turgid wall of brown water.

Is anything ever that simple? At least it was safe. Perfectly legal. Hadn't our two governments, tired of continual bickering and bloodshed, at last come to terms and settled by treaty the fate of these chunks of chopped-off ground, these "cut-offs" or *bancos* as the Boundary Commission calls them?

That was eighteen months ago, 1905, as who should know better than myself, Bancroft Benson, twenty-seven last May, an accomplished geologist who, startled by a glimpse of the great Main Chance, had a good many moons ago—two floods, as time is measured on the River—quit his underpaid job with the Topographical Survey to sweat here in leisure while frustratedly waiting for the bloody Rio Grande to make his goddam fortune.

If this sounds a bit steamed up, consider a few of the relevant facts. From El Paso to Boca Chica I had followed its hundreds of twists and meanderings with the assiduous persistence of a starving gadfly. Such dogged perseverance had been bound to turn up something. The trick, of course, had been to find the right levels and a piece of ground with enough improvements to be worth the bother.

Well, I found it. Seven hundred and some odd acres of prospective *banco*, replete with holdings worth an Inca's ransom, and all in the hands of a senile old rooster who had no more sense than a one-legged woodchuck. A principality, no less—the Hacienda Villalobos; white walls and red tiled roofs, the pink bell tower of the church with its cross gleaming through the lace of wind-tossed branches, the lush green of irrigated peon-worked fields standing out like new-sown patches against the lemon range. All this—and no telling how many hundreds of foraging cattle—waiting to fall right into my lap when the river, as one day it must, should gouge a new channel and make this a part of the United States.

Easy as eating striped candy.

To clothe my position with an appearance of legality I had first to become a bonafide land owner. Since I hadn't much cash and on the American side all the ground was pre-empted, I was forced to concede the necessity of a partner. The cowman who claimed the footage I needed was hardly the sort to be talked out of anything. I had to find someone who could obtain the ground for me.

I was exceedingly reluctant to split such a plum. I went back to the treaty, hoping to find a way around this impasse. What I found was another snag—a bad one. Ownership, by agreement, was to remain in the hands of the erstwhile occupants, whether Mexican or *Yanqui*; these being at liberty to retain or change their status.

I had supposed the land would be up for grabs.

Discovering the truth was a nasty jolt. All that time and labor wasted. Then I got to thinking. This feudal baron, Alfredo the Magnificent, was a doddering old fool who must have been in his seventies. What would he know about law! Throw a big enough fright, he wouldn't stop long enough to grab up his hat!

Somewhat reassured, I was now in the mood to consider a partner—better half a loaf than none. But it would have to be someone who could pull his weight. That was when I began to really think about Dorrus, the man on the ground, the bullypuss cowman I'd been figuring to buy out. He seemed rough enough and he was certainly no fool.

He made that apparent in mighty short order. "Partnership!" The whites of his eyes rolled back like a bronc's. "What the devil would I want with a partner!"

He folded thick arms across the breadth of his chest, unreadably watching through the smoke dribbling up from the tattered inch of butt sticking out of his mouth corner. "You got somethin' to offer."

"No cash," I said, glancing around distastefully.

His look got a little testy. "College feller, ain'tcha? They must work all you sports through the same piece of wire. Hellity larrup! You got somethin' to say, say it!"

Like a bear he stood in that black wool shirt with the snags of his teeth fastened into that stogie, both ears chopped off the way his kind mark cattle.

I didn't care about that, nor that his name was

Shirl Dorrus. It meant nothing to me. All I wanted was a base of operations and the kind of a partner I could get some mileage out of. I didn't care if the both of them stunk like shoats. "How much of this ground have you got under title?"

He rolled the soggy butt across the crack of his mouth.

"I'm not talking," I said, "just to hear my teeth rattle."

"You ain't cuttin' me off from water, sport. I got the whole goddam shore plastered far as you can see!" His look was like twin splinters of glass. "More to the point," and now he grinned, "I got this," he said, and slapped a fist around the grip of his pistol.

I grinned, too. "Would you swap for half of what's across the river?"

The pulpy weed disappeared behind the stumps of his teeth. His jaws got to grinding. Finally he spat. "You been out too long in that goddamn sun."

The gruff bark of his words was loaded with scorn. There was disgust in it, too, an underlying growl so crammed with resentment a child could have seen the greed tramping through it.

Some of my excitement likely showed in my grin. "If you're not interested," I said, "I can probably make out to find someone who is."

"Hell's fire!" he exploded in a violent shout.

"Man would have to be a goddamn fool to swaller that!"

"All right." I headed for the door.

I hadn't taken three steps when he caught my arm. The strength of his grip was astonishing. With no effort at all he spun me about. I went slamming into a hide-bottomed chair.

He looked confused, enraged, glowering over me like some chest-thumping ape. With surprise and alarm it came into my thinking this fellow could be dangerous. I pushed it aside. He was so eager to be persuaded it was almost laughable. His sort of tame wolf was just what I needed.

"I can get that place—"

"Villalobos?"

"The closest chunk of it," I nodded. "Something over seven hundred acres, and it isn't going to cost either one of us a dime."

He wasn't convinced, but it was evident enough he wanted to be. It stood out all over him. In the spraddle of his legs, in the huge locked lumps of those murderous fists, in the fierceness leaping from the glitter of his stare.

He made an effort to get hold of himself, moving back. "Talk's cheap," he snarled, irritably rasping both hands across his pantslegs. "Man don't cut up that kinda melon without he's got himself into a bind. If you ain't just yappin' you got a damn good reason—"

"Certainly I've a reason."

"Yeah. You need help!"

I let go of my jaw in a pretense of astonishment. I felt like saying, "How'd you guess?" but sarcasm on him would be breath wasted. He growled, eyes bright with suspicion, "I won't have no part in layin' hold of that skirt!"

"Ransom?" I laughed.

"Well . . . I don't want no run-in with them Rurales, neither!"

I couldn't help grinning. "The Mexican police won't come into this at all."

"Mebbe you think he'll wrap a pink ribbon round it? Sport, you're ready for a string of spools if you're hopin' that old bastard'll just up an' move out!"

"If we play our cards right he won't have much choice."

With his scowl getting darker he pushed that around. "Then it's got to be the girl. You want my place so you can strike up an acquaintance . . ."

I said sharper than I'd aimed to, "I'm not the marrying kind, you fool!"

He stomped around. He came back, looking ugly. "Then put it on the line, you son of a bitch, where I can see it!"

II

There were a number of things I might have done, but this was the guy I would have to do business with. I hung onto my temper. I could put up with considerable for half of Villalobos.

I made myself smile.

"What you want is the third step, partner. We'll progress a lot faster if we take things in turn—and you might just as well come unstuck from that pistol. You're in. We both know it. We both ought to know, too, I'm silly enough to turn loose of any facts until you're committed and I have adequate protection."

He stood with his head tipped, looking me over. "Pertection for what?"

"The operative word, friend, is *from,*" I said, "and I imagine you can figure out the answer to that."

He did some more staring and, abruptly, snorted. "How you reckon to git that pertection?"

"Why, there's nothing very difficult about it. Not really."

"Goin' to trot it around so I can watch the way its feet lifts?"

There is something recklessly improvident or brashly conceited about the way the great most of us deal with other people, taking them for granted, scarcely more than half seeing them. When I'd been scouting this proposition, considering the situation from those hills off yonder through a collapsible Army telescope, I had seen the old don and his high chinned daughter any number of times; yet the thing Shirl Dorrus had just put into my head hadn't ever once occurred to me.

I got to wondering why it hadn't. The girl was not unshapely. Though a bachelor from choice, I had a good enough opinion of my abilities with women not to feel any great concern with regard to the probable outcome. Nor would I be burdened, proceeding toward my goal through means of wedlock, with the necessity of sharing my coveted plum. In the fullness of time I'd have all of Villalobos, chattels, cattle—everything. And I'd not have to rub elbows with a swine like Shirl Dorrus. I couldn't think why the idea was repugnant. It wasn't as though I'd be chained to the woman.

"I'm still listenin'," he said, thumbs hooked into the dark shine of his belt.

Breaking away from my thoughts I peered a long time at him. "Well, the first step, of course . . . we'll have to go see a lawyer. Papers drawn up and signed."

"Why couldn't I just give you use of the place?"

"Whatever's worth doing is worth doing right." It was the things in my head I was seeing, not him. "You couldn't afford to have me backing out later. A binding agreement with the place changing hands for one dollar and 'other valuable considerations'—a transaction we can publicize. The property has got to be signed over."

"You think I'm a goddam idjit!" Dorrus shouted.

Outrage palely quivered in his stare. Anger fought with greed and lost. Distrust came out of him like a smell.

"You're not willing," I said, "to relinquish this worn-out hog run for half—?"

"You didn't need me by Gawd you wouldn't be here!"

"The fact is self-evident."

"Then don't act like I'm dirt under your feet!"

I stared at him astonished. This ignorant back country brush-popping bravo appeared to have needs I hadn't considered. He aspired to dignity! The poor slob wanted to be treated as an equal. I almost laughed before I realized he was serious.

Curbing my distaste I brought out my Burlington watch and cut a glance at it. "Very well," I smiled, "we'll be gents anyway till the balloon comes down. As business associates—"

"What I wanta know is what's to pertect me!"

"Another signed paper," I said, very patient. "Deposited, sealed, with the lord high sheriff or attorney general, to be opened in the event of your demise or disappearance. And you'll stay on as foreman. I should think that would give you assurance enough."

It was his turn to grin. A gray shine of satisfaction crept over the bulge of his beard stubbled cheeks. He bit off a crunch of repulsive twist dug from the clutter of a sweaty hip pocket. His look turned crafty. "An' what if I say the place is worth more?"

"You come in on my terms or you don't come in."

He glared, incensed. "If we're pardners," he whined, "we oughta be pardners straight acrost the board."

"Take it or leave it."

A child could have seen he didn't much like it, and it was plain enough he didn't like me. But I held top cards and he was shrewd enough to know this. The stumps of his teeth went to work on his cud while those pale piggish eyes through his seething suspicions continued, greed driven, to pick and to pry.

Still scowling, he nodded. "All right, sport, I'll take it."

We set off for the county seat in his buckboard.

Through the first twenty miles he never opened his mouth except to get rid of the juice from his chew. He had reckoned to go on the back of a horse but, in addition to wanting him where I could see him, I'd stood out for the wheels to let him know who was boss. It hadn't set well with him; he was still champing on it, along with the rest of the things he didn't like. Even when we stopped to blow the team he stayed hunched in his sullen silence. I made no attempt to josh him out of it, having enough problems of my own to keep track of.

How much should I tell him when the time came to do it? How much dared I tell?

I guess we probably made quite a picture, both of us clamped to that narrow seat, banging around like two eggs in hot water, fuming and fretting, sour with distrust, each of us bent to gain and keep the upper hand.

"If we should happen to bump into any folks you're acquainted with, be sure," I said, "to let them know you've sold out. The name is Bancroft Benson. Use it when you tell them to shake hands with the new owner."

He spat over the dash, still holding his spleen locked behind his bad teeth. "You're free to think whatever you care to," I said to him coolly, "but when we're around other people you'll behave as behooves a hired hand, mister, or find yourself tramping down the road."

The man's eyes widened. His breath sucked in and everything about him seemed to bunch and tighten. In that smoldering fury his affronted glance seemed almost to have the weight of a club. I could hear the grind of his jaws, and he yelled, “What’s to keep me from dumpin’ you out right here?”

“Greed,” I said, grinning back at him thinly. “You couldn’t stand to be left looking on so long’s there’s a chance I might pull this off. Here’s your dollar,” I said, and dropped it into his lap.

He started with his look growing darker and wilder. Wind rushed past the snarl of his teeth and with a sound of frustration he snatched up the whip and tore into the horses, lashing them into a headlong run.

It was pretty near ten when we picked up the lights of the county seat. The hotel dining room was closed for the night. There was an all-night hash house on the corner of Main just across from the courthouse. I went in and ordered while he was putting up the team. There were no other customers.

Well, I thought, so far so good. By tomorrow at this time, for one silver dollar, I stood to be down on the county’s books as bonafide owner of the Running Bee, a three-man outfit boasting some three hundred head of longhorn cattle and about ten miles of Rio Grande shoreline.

Sure I felt good—why wouldn’t I? There were still a few wrinkles to shake out of this blanket but at least I’d made a start. To build even this much out of nothing but words . . .

This much? I scowled. Bluffing others a man

might get by with, but the fellow who tries to kid himself is bound to be the shortest road for grief. The only smart thing I'd done was discover Villalobos, and already I was down to giving half of it away!

I pushed the thought aside. This deal was strewn with imponderables. The last chip wasn't yet out of my pocket. I might get lucky. If no one had dropped a wrench in the works two carloads of horses would be around this town someplace, waiting with papers for me to take delivery. Tomorrow I'd be in the driver's seat. A lot could happen before that river climbed out of its banks to put Villalobos into my backyard.

Shirl Dorrus tramped in on the rowels of his spurs, cut a swift look around and plopped himself down clear across the room. It was a childish defiance; but his kind, given an inch, would soon be reaching for a mile. Trying to hide my annoyance I got off my stool and, leaving the counter, went reluctantly over.

A jeering grin cleaved the snaggle of beard. He booted out a chair. "Take the weight off your feet. We got some augerin' to do."

I said, still standing, "This is no place to discuss private business."

"You'll discuss this, sport." There was in Shirl Dorrus a fat streak of aggressiveness, and something apparently had propped up his confidence. His look turned unpleasant.

The waitress appeared with her hands full of dishes. “Where do you want this food put, mister?”

“Right here,” Dorrus said. “And fetch me the same.”

She wheeled over and put my dinner on his table. When she left I said to him, “What are you after?”

“A fair shake, Benson.”

“Shirl,” I said, “you’ve got a fair shake.”

“Looks pretty skimpy from my end of the stick. Too one-sided. I want some insurance.”

“You’re already covered.”

“Then cover me some more. I don’t want no drafts blowin’ down my neck, an’ I don’t want this dido blowin’ up in my face.”

“You needn’t worry about that.”

His grin came back. “What I been tellin’ myself. Fine upstandin’ young feller like you would be sure as hell wantin’ to do the right thing.”

I had time to observe the thinness of the silence and, behind that fish-mounted look, to see the shine of satisfaction building up like gas inside him. The excitement here went beyond what was reasonable.

While I was trying to set my finger on the source, the fellow’s gloat-roughened voice, fierce with pleasure, declared, “When I pass that shyster the deed to my place you’ll hand over a writin’ with yer John Henry on it that—whenever

I want it, without let or hendrance—will split me off half of everything you got." Filled with triumph he cried, "You'll do this, sport, or you got no deal!"

III

Bluff.

Of course!

It had to be bluff, I thought, grayly staring.

But if I attempted to call . . . if I swung round and walked out of this place—and he let me, I'd be under his thumb like a chunk of milk toast.

Because I'd have to come back. There was no way around him. Even if I could wrap up money enough it was too late now to buy out Shirl Dorrus; the extent of his importance was beginning to impress him. To fatten my claims against Don Alfredo I needed that shoreline, and to acquire it I had to deal with Dorrus.

I wished to God I never had heard of him!

"All right," I growled, sitting down to my food, doing the best I could to conceal my turmoil. "I'll think about it, anyway."

"You do that, sport."

I didn't have to look up to catch the sly grin. The smug bloat of his tone was insufferable enough. I chewed in a glower of castrated fury, envisioning a dozen dire things which could be figured to release me from the yoke of his tyranny. Then, in the midst of these impossible imaginings, I saw what my own greed had done.

In my desire to convince him I had been too clever. Now my hands were tied, tied by the very means I had used to reassure him. He was safe, all right; he was in this for half no matter how much I hated it.

We shared a room at the Texas House—his idea, not mine. We had breakfast together in the hotel dining room, and together we went and sat with a lawyer while he drew up articles of partnership which we signed in front of him and a notary and a couple of barflies he called in to witness it. When we got through with that lawyer there was no doubt in anyone's mind that we were not only partners, but equal partners in anything either of us had or might acquire.

Shirl Dorrus, buttoning away his copy of the agreement, was feeling pretty expensive when we finally got out of there. We had signed three copies, the third to be held by the lawyer for probate at whatever time the decease of either partner should make such action mandatory.

No more than we reached the street Dorrus said, "Now that we've got our obligations took care of I'm rarin' to hear how we part Villalobos from that bunch of damned greasers."

"Villalobos," I said shortly, "wasn't mentioned in that agreement."

His mouth fell open. His eyes looked like they might roll off his cheekbones. His jaws slammed shut, flung wide again in the outraged bellow of a goaded bull.

He grabbed for his hip but I was there before him, stepping clear with his pistol, dumping the loads from it, throwing it back at him. He caught it awkwardly, off balance, red-faced and snarling, clumsy with fury.

I said to him sharply, "Shooting down a partner who doesn't pack a gun is a pretty good way to fit a rope around your neck. You'd better give some thought to those papers you just signed."

I left him glaring at me speechless and moved toward the bank. I heard the strike of his spurs coming through the door after me. Ignoring him completely I went over to the cashier's wicket and said to the bald head behind the grille, "My name is Bancroft Benson." He stepped to the back of his cage and summoned a clerk who, after listening, nodded and hurried off out of sight. The cashier smiled. "Did you have a good trip?"

"Good enough," I said, finding Dorrus at my elbow fairly bristling with suspicion.

The bald head said, "Pardon me. Something for you, sir?"

"I'm with him," Dorrus growled; and then a dignified gentleman with a considerable stomach and a grizzle of whiskers along the sides of the face came out of a door that was gold-lettered PRIVATE and, moving up, caught my hand.

Smiling, he said, "Mr. Benson—a pleasure. I'm Horace Finchbone. Will you step into my office?"

"I'm a little pressed for time just now. I've purchased the Running Bee from Mr. Dorrus here who's consented to stay on for a while as my range boss. You have my funds?"

Finchbone nodded. "All your instructions have been followed to the letter. You may draw on us at will."

"Thank you. A block of checks, I think, will do for the nonce."

Bald head pushed one through his wicket. Mr. Finchbone, smiling, put it into my hands. "Have a good trip?"

"A bit dusty," I said, slipping the checks inside my suitcoat.

"Well," the manager sighed with a somewhat distasteful glance at Dorrus, "we're glad to see fresh blood coming in." His stare went obliquely over Dorrus again. He smoothed his weskit, dredged up another smile. "I hope you'll be happy here."

Outside Dorrus growled, "What was that all about?"

"He doesn't appear to have you on the same shelf with Moses. We'll step over to the courthouse," I said, and struck out for it.

His arm lunged up as though to lay hold of me. Instead he slammed his hat on the ground. He said fiercely, “God damn it! If you got money in there—”

Since I hadn’t stopped to listen I didn’t catch the rest of it. Wheezing, spluttering, looking about to bust his surcingle, he overhauled me just as I started up the steps. “I got rights!” he shouted, swelled up like a carbuncle.

I said, “When you start living up to your part of our agreement—when you act like a hired hand instead of a fishwife, I might be inclined to consider your reproaches.”

Without waiting for any more of his guff, I pushed into the place, finding at the end of a door lined corridor the entrance marked RECORDER’S OFFICE.

A sallow faced clerk in sleeve guards and garters was poring over a ledger that took up two yards of the counter. “My name is Bancroft Benson,” I told him. “I am here to record a transfer of property.”

The clerk, exercising the prerogatives of his kind, was apparently of the opinion I could give all day to the business. Reaching over the counter I got a fistful of shirtfront. Thus made aware of me he tried to pull loose. When his efforts proved ineffectual the myopic eyes behind his steel-rimmed spectacles took on the bulge of a frightened rabbit’s.

“Think you can hear me now?” I said.

Not able to swallow the clerk bobbed his head.

By this time Dorrus, jaws locked, stood beside me. I let go of the fellow. I laid my bargain and sale deed on the counter in front of him. "I want this recorded. I want the transfer entered in your books. Now get at it."

He snatched up the paper and scuttled off.

"What the hell's the big sweat?" Dorrus growled, keeping his voice down. "You've already got title—"

The clerk came back after a while and pushed my deed across the counter. There were tax stamps affixed to it and, at the top of the front fold, a rubber-stamped file number and a series of initials in a box across the bottom. There was also the date, a notary seal and the recorder's signature. "Fine," I said, and carefully put it away. "Now post your ledger so it will show the transfer."

"We don't post the ledgers."

"You're posting this."

He worked up quite a glare but it kind of played out on him. Muttering under his breath he grabbed up a pen, got down another ledger, slapped over some pages and, looking like a mouse with its tail in a crack, began an angry scribbling. I watched over his shoulder. When he flung down the pen I nodded. We left.

"I can see," Dorrus grumbled as we came back on the street, "this ain't just somethin' you scratched outa thin air." A puzzled resentment banged around through his tone. "Finchbone put you up to this, sport?"

"What difference would that make?"

"Son of a bitch would skin a flea." He rolled bitter eyes at me. "How much of a stake has he got in this dido—you can tell me that, can'tcha?"

"No stake at all. He's got nothing to do with it."

Keeping step with me, scowling, Dorrus presently said, "You musta done considerable figgerin' to put money in his hands before you ever come near here." He peered at me slanchways. The stab of his stare held a grudging respect. "How much would you have give fer my place if you'd had to?"

I could almost have laughed at so ridiculous a thought. When I paid for the horses I had ordered set down here I wouldn't have over forty dollars to my name. Let him think what he wanted. There was no scope for profit in explaining this to Dorrus. I scraped up a smile. "Can't you be satisfied, Shirl, with half of Villalobos?"

"I ain't got even half a calf from it yet!" The sulky planes of his cheeks, the edgey-tempered turmoil leaching from the yeasty churn of his thoughts, was a foretaste, it looked like, of what lay in store for me.

But sufficient to the moment is the evil thereof. I pushed the nag of this aside. I had troubles enough without borrowing problems I might never be faced with.

Dorrus came abruptly out of his brooding to throw a hard look about. “What the hell,” he said, “are we comin’ out here fer?”

We were crossing the tracks. I said, “Aren’t those pens a part of the stockyards?”

His mouth flattened out. “You dealin’ them stockyard bums in, too?”

“We’re taking delivery on two carloads of horses.”

“Horses!” He stared. “We got more broncs now than we’re like t’ find feed fer!”

“There’ll be feed for these. What’s out there now I’m getting rid of,” I said.

IV

Though I had not actually addressed myself to the matter, it had crossed my mind that one of these days, in his work upon the range, an act of Providence or something might take him off my back. Rattlesnake or gopher hole. Some happily murderous cow brute, maybe. In this kind of country the possibilities were infinite. A slipping girth, a broken neck. An avalanche. A falling rock.

Such comforting visions were no longer feasible. That shyster we'd been to had cut their throats before I'd hardly grasped his purpose. The partnership papers he'd kept "for probate" had ruled out any such fortuitous solution. I was yoked to Shirl Dorrus tighter than Damon had been to Pythias. A Mexican standoff. With those papers hanging over us neither he nor I could afford to let Death set him up as the survivor. It would appear too much of a coincidence, Don Alfredo's hacienda too obviously involved.

There were, however, certain small satisfactions I might safely indulge. This was an ignorant man; I could maneuver him. So long as the means for acquiring Villalobos remained beyond his ken, I held the whip hand. His ranch was in my name and, while his unstable temper made him difficult—even dangerous, the greed I'd brought to the fore was a handle, a bar and barrier behind which a man of wit should be able to achieve quite a number of things.

"Before you throw your nose out of joint," I said calmly, "you had better consider the facts of this business. If it gets out we're partners the whole show will fold. This you had better believe and keep in mind, Shirl." I surveyed him grimly. "We have a good thing going but its feasibility, all the salient features, hinge irrevocably on the image of myself as master of Running Bee. We're done, stopped cold, if anything—mind you, the least breath of suspicion."

"Why, by God, don't you talk plain American!"

"If you want kindergarten words these horses I've shipped in are part of the stage dressing, props we're using to make the illusion of my ownership more real. A clean sweep, Shirl. We get rid of everything."

His chin shot out. "Not my cattle!"

"Whose cattle? Be reasonable, man. I've bought this place. I'll do anything I want with it. The more we can change it the more convincing it will seem. We're pulling down those flea coops. We'll put up a new house, new stables, corrals—something impressive, more in keeping with the notions of a gentleman horse breeder."

I saw the lips wrench back off his rotten teeth. "By God!" His eyes were like two slivers of glass. “If I reckoned fer a minute this was nothin’ but a stunt t’ do me outa Runnin’ Bee.”

“Don’t talk like a bleating idiot! At the worst all you’ve lost is some hardscrabble range that by your own say-so is about grazed out. I’m the one ought to be hollering, putting myself in your hands like I have! You get half of anything I ever lay hold of. Gobs of fire! What more do you want?”

“Somethin’ I can feel,” he said, “somethin’ that can’t lie!”

“You’ve got Bancroft Benson hitched to a treadmill, tied hand and foot—read it, man!” I considered him testily. Yet riled as I was I hadn’t quit thinking. Here was my chance to point up the teeth in it. “Shirl,” I said, “do you realize where I would be if something happened to you and these papers turned up? They’d have me kicking at the end of a rope! That agreement I signed covers you like a tent.”

He scowled, undecided. “That cuts both ways.”

“I should hope so,” I told him. This was the clinker I’d been driving the talk at. “If I turn up my toes they put the necktie on you. What they call an ‘umbrella’—a pretty good inducement for staying on the level. There are other facets you’d do well to keep in sight. Nothing’s really foolproof; you might get around it but the law takes a pretty dim view of flight. The man who runs—”

"I can see through a winder! You don't hev t' mash my nose a'gin' it!"

"Just so we know where we stand," I told him. Then I saw his look tighten. A slyness crept into it. "If we're pardners," he said, "it looks like to me I should git half of them checks."

I considered him, flabbergasted. Patiently I said, "The fact that we're partners is the one thing, Shirl, we—"

"You can git around that. You told Fishbone I'm yer range boss. You can fix it up with him fer me to draw—"

"He'd consider that mighty queer, I'm afraid. Besides," I said, "time we've paid for these horses I won't have more than forty dollars in the bank."

Dorrus' cheeks grew dark. His eyes turned ugly. "All them big ideas," he snarled, "what you figgerin' t' use fer money?"

"Far as it will go I'm counting on using what I get for the cattle and broomtails already on the ground." I'd no intention of standing around arguing the matter. "If it takes more than that," I said, "we'll borrow it."

The horses, as promised, were penned up and waiting. Two fellows in range clothes, chewing and whittling, sat on the top rail of the nearest corral. Until I spoke they paid no visible attention to anything beyond the steady bite of their knives. I looked the stock over. "Either of you fellows connected with these horses?"

"What about 'em?" the younger one said, glancing up.

"If they're billed to Bancroft Benson they're mine."

The youngster—sandy-haired, blue-eyed and freckled—tossed down his stick, put away his knife and clasped both arms about a drawn-up knee. "These here broncs, until they're paid for, is Three Ds, accordin' to what I been told. You Benson?"

"That's right," I nodded.

"You got anything to prove it?"

I looked at the kid, and at the older hand with him. It got no change out of either one. "Shirl," I said, ignoring his scowl, "tell these fellows who I am."

The youngster said, "That wouldn't help none. I don't know him, either."

Unwinding, the youngster dropped off his high perch, stepping around to the right of us. At the same time the other hand moved up on our left.

Even Dorrus turned still.

The cold of dread began to creep through my stomach, knowing Shirl's temper and the need bottled in him to strike out at something.

Blue-Eyes said, watching both of us: "Expect my boss might not be too tickled, but these kind of ponies don't get broke from the brush at the snap of a finger." It was about as near as he could come to an apology. It didn't warm up the cut of his stare. "If either of you gents can prove to me you're Benson—"

"Button," Dorrus lipped, "you've bit off more'n you can chew."

"Shirl, be still!" I cried, trying to scout a safe way through this. That kid wasn't going to back down one inch; he stood braced for trouble like a dog with lifted hackles. The last thing I wanted here or any place was gunplay. "Would a banker's identification satisfy you?"

Blue-Eyes, pushing it around, tentatively nodded. "Tap," he said, "sashay over to the bank and see if you can get a description of Benson."

The older hand trotted off without so much as a backward glance. It was pretty impressive. I'd been inclined to suggest we all tag along, that while we were over there I'd write out a check for him. I left the words unsaid.

He twisted a smoke, blue-eyes playing over us cool as a well chain. He wasn't about to walk off from these bangtails.

I cleared my throat. "I got the impression, from my talk with Waggoner's foreman, there'd be mostly Travelers in this bunch and something he referred to, I believe, as 'dust' horses. Does that make sense?"

"Everything we left with is here," the youngster said. "If they're yours I'll point 'em out to you."

With wide lips flexing noncommittally, he lifted a match to his smoke, afterward breaking it between two fingers before letting it drop into the heavy yellow dust.

Shirl Dorrus snorted. I was not able to dismiss the fellow so lightly. I could not help feeling, despite his youth and histrionics, I was looking at a highly capable man. Frankly one I would prefer to step around if he would let me.

The quiet piled up, broken presently by the approaching clump of boots. I glanced around at the sound and saw the man who had left coming up in the wake of the bearded banker. Finchbone, peering questioningly at me, introduced himself somewhat pompously to Blue-Eyes. The youth heard him out, saying only in return, "You know this gent?"

Finchbone peered around at me again. "He has an account at my bank in the name of Bancroft Benson."

The youngster, considering me, chewed on that through several moments of silence. "Will it cover an obligation of fifteen hundred dollars?"

Finchbone appeared somewhat startled, I thought, but declared vigorously enough that he imagined it would.

The young fellow nodded. "These horses," he said, "are from the Waggoner ranch and set down here for Bancroft Benson, collect on delivery. If the bank's satisfied this gent is Benson I'll take a cashier's check and we'll consider them delivered."

It was the banker's turn to re-examine his position. He said, a little sharply, "No need going to all that bother. He's good for the amount."

"I'm sure he is," the young fellow smiled. "So I'll take the bank's check and we'll consider the matter settled."

V

If all the Waggoner hands were as sharply shrewd as this blue-eyed cuss the outfits' future would have been assured even without the lake of oil their drills had gone into while they'd been trying to scare up water for their cattle.

That cold-jawed youngster didn't want any part of us, not even at double the going rate. Soon as he'd got the bank's draft in his jeans he allowed the horses were mine and washed his hands of them. He did point out the five which were Steeldusts, waxing quite eloquent about the bloodlines and abilities of the coal-black stallion he said was Tom Rock. But that was the size of it. He wouldn't even help line them out toward the ranch. We finally wound up hiring a couple of hands we dug out of a saloon.

Tom Rock was the only stallion I'd purchased. There were five chunky geldings, the rest mares and colts. The geldings were what he described as "green broke." The rest of those hides hadn't even been curried. It took us six days, living off the land, to get them in sight of the Running Bee.

Dorrus helped, sour and sarcastic, what time he wasn't openly throwing fits about "all that money" I had poured down a rat hole. He couldn't seem to get over it. "Damned if I can figger you," he'd growl. "Fifteen hundred throwed plumb away on a ragtag of broomies that wouldn't bring fifty dollars set right down at the glue factory! Jesus H. Christ!"

If he said it once he must have said it thirty times. Every time we stopped for grub he said it, variously embellishing it according to the whim and temper of the moment. "If you'd on'y told me what you was up to," he declared at least twice. "I coulda saved you half of it an' corraled enough whickers to've cornered the market! Godfreys, Benson, what the bloody hell good are they?"

Once, when I ventured to remark that they were pretty, he got to swearing so furious I looked for him to strangle. "I give in they're pretty," he snarled when he got back to talking. "A polecat's pretty, but what kinda fool would give fifteen hundred to surround hisself with 'em! If we git down, by God, t' havin' t' eat 'em, you won't git more'n ten cents on the dollar!"

Most of the time I just let him rant. He certainly convinced the barflies we'd hired. They obviously believed I'd been "took" bad as the guy toting sack for snipe. By the time we got them corraled on the place I was beginning to wonder myself how big a fool I'd been.

It didn't matter to me that I knew nothing about horses; I could stay on their backs if they weren't too wild, and I suspected that would be sufficient for my purpose. I had not purchased them to impress Shirl Dorrus. The Ybarras, Spaniards of the old school, were most likely of the persuasion no one but a horseman should converse with important people, the horse being accepted as the hallmark of a gentleman. These caste signs, in dealing with a *hacendado*, could prove the deciding factor. For this reason I had been at some considerable pains to make certain the horse end of my background was worthy of his attention.

I cannot think why I was so determined to seem socially acceptable to the man I planned to rob. Taken at face value it must appear an aberration, some facet of vanity, for it was the river, remember, on which I was counting to put Villalobos within reach of Shirl's pistol. Alfredo's thoughts and his daughter had nothing to do with this compulsion; yet it was there, an aching molar which had prodded me into no little inquiry, this in turn resulting in my deal with the Waggoners. Perhaps somewhere at the back of my thinking I was seeking a second string for my bow. I refused irascibly to look any closer. The stallion, Tom Rock, was descended from a line of colonial all-purpose stock which two centuries ago the Chickasaw Indians had run up out of Florida, at that time known as Spanish Guale. He was the scion of a particular and peculiar relatively modern strain established in this line by the stallion Steel Dust, with which one Mid Perry had bankrupted an entire Texas county. They were speed horses.

I had secured Tom's pedigree when I'd talked with the Waggoner foreman. Tom Rock was by Rocky Mountain Tom who was sired by Pid Hart. Pid Hart was by Shelby, he by Tom Driver, by Steel Dust out of Mammoth, she by Shyloe. Dam of Rocky Mountain Tom was Lady Gladys, she by Bill Garner, he by Steel Dust. Pid Hart's dam was Jennie Capps, she by Dash. First dam of Lady Gladys was Mancoe's big filly, she by Little Bert, dam by the Old Mancoe roan race mare. Fast getaway and terrific velocity over short distances was as common to this stock as horns are to cattle, according to Waggoner's foreman.

Tom Rock's dam was a blood bay by Eureka by Shelby, second dam Mattie Stephens (also the dam of Shelby and of the celebrated Governor Roberts), by Shyloe out of Nellie Gray, she by Dan Secres, he by Old Joe Chalmers, the celebrated four-mile horse owned by Capt. Tom Haley. Dan Secres' dam was Mary Cook by Printer, which last went direct to imported Janus, a four-mile horse on the English turf.

These horses, as I have already noted, were bred in speedy bloodlines. Rocky Mountain Tom twice defeated Panzareta, the famous Trammell race mare, current holder of the World's Record for five-eighths of a mile. He was a lap-and-tap brush horse with tremendous early foot. I was counting heavily on Tom Rock—my stallion—having inherited some of this.

He stood fifteen hands and weighed about twelve hundred. Steel Dust, I'd been told, had been a little taller, a blood bay of approximately the same weight. Tom Rock was four years old, broken to the saddle but still unraced. He was a fine looking animal, remarkable for roundness of contour, strength of articulation, indicating great powers in his whole conformation. Compact, he was, with extra powerful hind legs and, in his eyes, the look of eagles.

I might have pointed out some of these things to Shirl Dorrus, perhaps to some extent mitigating the scornful contempt he took every opportunity of displaying toward the outlay of cash I'd put into this stock. As it happened I kept the knowledge to myself. This way, if things didn't pan out, I would not be reproached on that basis at least. I was becoming by now, heartily sick of Shirl Dorrus and all his works.

I hadn't considered in town that we would really need help; back there fourteen horses hadn't seemed such a much for two grown men to manage. Dorrus had thrown up his hands in towering contempt when Blue-Eyes remarked we'd need at least two helpers. It had been mainly to irritate Shirl that I'd hired them. Before we got home I would have gladly had six.

What took us so long was mainly attributable to the contrary notions of that black devil, Tom Rock. He figured to take care of this "menatha" himself and apparently imagined it his sole prerogative. Town was still in sight when he ran off the five geldings. He was finally made to know he had to put up with them, but he wouldn't let them anywhere near his mares. He had plenty of lung power and a fine set of teeth, both of which he used to remarkable effect.

This much we could have managed to abide. What really frayed our tempers was his determined persistence to take charge of the drive and, as though this were not cross enough for us to bear, his repeated attempts to take off with our stock horses in every direction but the one that would bring us to Running Bee. At least half of our time was spent fetching them back. We never rode less than fifteen miles to gain five. There were times I didn't think I could take another minute of it. If Dorrus had been permitted he would have shot Tom out of hand.

I've lost count of the times we flared up at each other, shouting and swearing like a couple of termagants. At one point I said, "I've got seven hundred dollars invested in that horse. You're not going to shoot him and you're not climbing onto him!" At another point Dorrus talked of putting him in hobbles.

It was mid-afternoon of the sixth day that we

caught a first welcome glimpse of the Rio. "At last!" I growled, letting out a great sigh. The ranch wasn't four miles off as the crow flies. Across the dun bluffs, the mesquites and cholla, you could see the bell tower and red tiles of Villalobos, with several twists of the river throwing back the white glare.

I was savoring the first free breath I had drawn in hours when Dorrus let out a shout, the stallion trumpeted and, tails up, the whole damned *manada* took off squealing for water.

Dorrus flung down his hat. "Let the sonsa-bitches go!"

VI

It was plain our barflies saw eye to eye with him. Nor could I honestly blame them. But I had too much tied up in those nags to sit like a nump while they went over some cliff—not, anyway, if there was chance to prevent it. "After 'em!" I shouted, waving my arms.

Nobody moved or bothered even to glance at me.

"Damn it!" I yelled, furious, and kicked my mount into a reluctant run, applying my spurs in reckless temper.

There was no possibility of overtaking them. All those extra miles we had squandered had left this dun in a pretty bad wilt. His jaw was flopping like a blacksmith's apron, but there was mustang enough in him that he would likely keep going until he fell in his tracks. One thing was for sure. If I would turn those broncs I had to find some way of being out on the bluffs ahead of them.

About a rope's length below where we had rimmed out, the slope fell away all broken and tumbled in a rock strewn slide perhaps a quarter mile long, ugly and treacherous as anything I'd seen. It was no time for thinking. I had this one chance, the only one in sight of beating them into that criss-cross of gullied brakes.

I did not stop to pick any daisies. The dun in

a stumbling run tried to swerve but the slap of my hat in his face forced him over. We dropped twelve feet like falling out of a windmill. When we struck my stomach was against the roof of my mouth and my spine felt like it had gone through my skull. For thirty yards, maybe, we tobogganed along on that bleating dun's rump and then, muscles surging, he tried to yank his legs out of it and, with a sudden fierce rumble, the ground started moving.

Never have I experienced anything like those next few moments. It seemed like the whole damned side of the hill had come loose. Wind and dust and a grinding roar and the jolting under us are all I remember. Somewhere between the top and the bottom, the dun, with a lunge and a scramble, must have freed himself, got onto all fours, because the next thing I knew the brakes were around us in a nightmare blur and he was bounding like a rabbit, trying to get out of it before all that rubble behind tore into us.

A gulch opened up on the right and he shot into it, crashing through brush like hell wouldn't have him. It clawed at my legs, ripped across my chest, but the dun kept going and, somehow, I managed to hang on and stay aboard him. Then the walls dropped behind and we were out in the open on a bench above the bluffs.

The dun, wild-eyed and shaking, stopped. I needed mightily to sigh but could not find breath enough. That slide must have moved with the speed of an express because the horses, when I twisted to look up, weren't much more than halfway down by the roundabout way Tom Rock was fetching them.

I did sigh then. There was still a possibility, if they came humping along as they were presently moving, I should be able to head and bend them across the top of the bluffs until we came onto some means of reaching the river that would not leave half of them dead or crippled. I might have trusted the stallion, but this was country he had never encountered and—with Shirl and the other two raising dust back of him—there was no telling what he might do.

The dun was still trembling.

He appeared to take a dim view of my signaled instructions and laid back his ears when I gave him the nudge. In no mood to put up with any more flimflam, I raked his flanks with the bite of my spurs.

The dun was still trembling.

To buck, a horse has to get his head down. When he found he couldn't, the old dunny took off, running sideways. Teeth bared, his head snaked around, the whites of his eyes clearly showing his intention. I snatched a leg out of reach and slammed my boot at his jaw. It straightened him out as nothing else could have, lifting him into a hard choppy run.

He was hurt, that was plain enough, hind legs not quite tracking. At another time, probably, I'd have had more regard for him. Right then the only picture I had was all that spent money at the bottom of some cliff.

I could see that at best it would be nip and tuck. Tom Rock and the mares were almost onto the bench, dropping into the brush just above it and still, by the looks, nearly twice that far ahead of me. I kept banging my rowels against ribs and hips. Now, desperate, I began swinging the rein ends. We gained a bit, held it, picked up a little more, then I felt him falter and start to come apart under me.

Only his bulldog heart kept him going. I thought my arms would be dragged from their sockets so great was the strain of holding his head up. It required every last ounce of strength I could summon, standing in the stirrups to get enough leverage, grayly knowing my last chance of stopping them was lost.

A hundred feet ahead, through a haze of despair, I could see my money spilling out across the shaley rim that, scarcely forty yards beyond, sheerly dropped to the cedar bottoms. I yelled in an agony of frustration, crazily shouting at the top of my lungs as the dun, wallowing under me, capsized in a loose-jointed fall.

I don't know whether it was the shouts torn, out of me or the sudden sharp crackle of gunfire racketing up from below but, even as I was flung from the saddle, I saw Tom Rock pull up and swerve.

Up again, bruised and badly shaken, I found the whole band vanishing hellity-larrup well back from the rim through a lemon dust as Shirl Dorrus and our hired pair swarmed out of the brush.

Dorrus peered at me queerly, then rode over to the rim.

“Be no broken legs now. They’re headed for the notch.”

“But what was that shooting?”

“Looks like some of Alfredo’s boys was down in the bottoms. Time that bunch gits to water they’ll hev ’em in a surround. All we gotta do then is ride up an’ claim ’em.” He looked at me and snorted. “There’s ten of them bastards. You figger we kin do it?”

VII

I stared in some alarm.

"You mean," I said, "they'd attempt to keep those horses?"

He looked, through his week's growth of straggly whiskers, as though I had asked who killed Cock Robin. He peeled the lips off his snags in a nasty grin. "C'mon," he said, "we'll damn soon find out!"

The two barflies, back of him, swapped worried scowls.

"Just a minute," I called. "What about this dun?"

He peered, wheeling over. "Guess you'll hev to git up behind . . ."

"Guess again," I said.

He pulled his chin up, staring. When he saw this hadn't improved things, he gruffly bade one of our hired sots to dismount.

"Surely," I said, gathering up the dropped reins, "you don't seriously suggest these people will imagine they can seize my horses?"

Dorrus, splattering tobacco juice, snorted. "You're the one with the crystal ball, sport. If you can't read it, don't look at me."

"You've neighbored with these Ybarras."

"Ha!" he said, and I climbed into the saddle.

"Near enough, leastways," he declared derisively, "to know better'n try t' prognosticate which way a damn pickle will most likely squirt!"

I watched the horseless barfly, muttering and mumbling, haul himself up behind his frowsy companion. It occurred to me to wonder, as we swung into Dorrus' wake, what arrangement of events could have inspired this kind of talk. Had he been feuding with the *hacienda*?

Considering what I knew of him, bad blood did not seem too farfetched an assumption. This was one of the things I had not thought to look into. I uncomfortably hoped their antipathy—if there was any—had not yet embraced bloodshed.

At least they were not shooting on sight.

This much was evident when, having dropped through the beat-up dust of the notch, we came out of cedar to behold our stock being loosely herded by several broad-cheeked horsebackers in disreputably floppy hats. Between these and ourselves, also mounted, four others with rifles across their pommels sat waiting.

I didn't wait for Dorrus to unlimber any argument. The blood pounding into his cheeks was all the notice I needed to clamp down on his arm. I said, "I'll do the talking," and reined out ahead of him.

The four sat their ponies as though cut from stone. One, darker jowled, more excitable than his companions and with a wart on his jaw, burly shouldered and solid, I took for the straw boss or *hacienda*'s chief *vaquero*. Most conspicuous of this group, if for no better reason that his outlandish length, was a loose-jointed jigger behind a ragged mustache whose blue stare appeared fixed with singular interest on a point which approximated Dorrus' position.

"Stay put," I said, and rode the last thirty feet in a quiet only broken by the footfalls of my mount.

I had no difficulty guessing which was Don Alfredo. The mark of the *rico* stamped every inch of him. Stout, big bellied, a person of obvious importance, so impeccably groomed he made me feel like a tramp.

In complete command of both himself and his manners, "*Buenas tardes, señor*," he said when I reined up before them.

"Good afternoon to you, sir," I nodded, a little resentful of my own poor appearance. Feeling somewhat dubious of any extended conversations in Spanish, but doing the best I could with the language, I named myself, mentioning that I had just purchased the land, good will and other assets of the Running Bee from the former owner, Shirl Dorrus, to all of which he listened without change of expression. When I added I would probably be keeping Dorrus on as range boss I thought the silence got a little more noticeable, and both his described companions mirrored this impression with the hardening of their stares.

Ybarra maintained his courtly composure. "But of course," he said. "And will you use the same brand?"

"I'll use a hoof brand, if any—a Double B Connected. I'm getting rid of those cattle. I'm a horse breeder," I told them, glancing casually across the dark-skinned straw boss' shoulder. "I see your boys are holding that bunch that just got away from me, and I thank you for your thoughtfulness."

"*Por nada*," he smiled, and then in English, "Please allow me to present myself. I am," he declared, inflating his chest, with a gesture embracing the distant shine of red tiles, "Alfredo Francisco Ybarra y Palacios—master of Villalobos. All that you see beyond the river is mine."

I couldn't help it. Pomposity always brings out the worst in me. "With such a clutter of possessions to look after," I remarked, "I'm surprised you would find any time left for trespassing."

It was stupid of me, inexcusable really. You could see the slap of it penetrate the armor of his self esteem, the affronted darkening of faces, the winkless inspection of the gaunt giant's pale stare. "My fault," the latter drawled, drawing a hand down over the brush of his mustache. "I wanted to try out a new saddle gun, and all the damned grouse seem to have flown over here."

Don Alfredo smiled indulgently, having apparently decided while the gawky one was flapping his jaw to credit my unhappy remark to gringo tactlessness. "This," he said now, indicating the tall one, "is my dear friend and guest, Don Patricio, who collects the *costumbres*—the what you call customs at El Paso del Norte."

We exchanged frosty looks from where we sat in our saddles, a kind of saturnine mirth coldly brightening his stare before, with a grunted "Pleasure," I dismissed him.

"And this," Ybarra said, extending an arm in the regal gesture of a prestidigitator about to conjure up his most cherished rabbit, "is my daughter, Linda."

She was the fourth of the group and had remained up till now more or less concealed behind the shoulders of the men. As the others made room to let her horse come through I got my first close-up look at a lady of quality.

She rode side-saddle, of course, and, contrary to my original impression that all four had rifles across their laps, was not armed. Despite the heat—and there was plenty of it, she was voluminously bundled in ankle-length skirts bespangled with braid to match the gold of her hair over which, in the Spanish fashion, piled high at the back with the aid of a comb, she had draped the blue lace of an elegant shawl. *Rebozo*, I believe, it was called around there.

She looked like something off a travel folder,

somewhat wilted, to be sure, but every whit as imperious and spoiled-brat disdainful as the remembered glimpses I had caught through the glass. And again I let temper stride roughshod over judgment.

Well aware of my unsavory appearance and pungent aroma after so long in the wilds without proper ablutions, yet determined to cut her down to size, I wedged my horse alongside her own and, in cruel mimicry of mores recently in vogue among our toplofty gentlemen, fetched her hand to my lips in a flamboyant flourish. Ridiculous and childish, as impudent almost as the grin with which I waited to be slapped.

To my considerable astonishment her strange eyes regarded me with pleasant surprise. Chagrined, I became rather more disgruntled to discover my prank appeared to have won a rather widespread approval. Behind his great beak and curly beard even her father's china teeth gleamed in a patina of gratified ego.

He thrust his rifle back into its boot and in a burst of staccato Spanish directed his straw boss to see that my outfit had help with the stock. "While they are driving the horses to your ranch," he said, "perhaps you will honor my poor house with your presence that we may become better acquainted over a little refreshment. Come—you are very welcome, my friend."

Since Dorrus looked mightily put out with the

suggestion, which obviously had not included him, I assured Don Alfredo I should be most happy to accept. Thus it happened that the four of us—Linda, Don Alfredo, the grouse hunting tax collector and myself—struck out for the *hacienda*, leaving a fortune in livestock at the mercy of menials.

Although not entirely at ease with this arrangement, such disquiet as I had was occasioned more by my distrust of Shirl Dorrus than by conjured fears of Spanish treachery. It was unthinkable that Ybarra at this stage of our acquaintance, and with never an untoward act to prompt it, should be contriving either to steal my property or plotting some inimical disadvantage to my person. I was actually looking forward with keen, even impatient, interest to an inside on-the-ground look at Villalobos.

Oddly enough, I found myself paired off with the girl. She was not as young, seen close up, as I'd imagined, most likely in her middle twenties, albeit uncommonly well preserved for this climate. That she was also perceptive I discovered very presently when out of a rather constrained silence she said, "I'm not like that, really," with her glance straight ahead.

"Like what?" I said, more to be polite than with any curiosity. As a matter of fact my thoughts were far afield, trying to gauge how much weather we were going to have to have to entice that river to get out of its banks and gouge the new channel that should give me her father's holdings.

"Like whatever you were thinking when you set out on the buffoonery of that ridiculous kiss."

Our eyes met and held. Though mentally wobbling from the shock her words had given me she had certainly captured every shred of my attention. With burning cheeks and disgust at having put myself in so ambiguous a position, unable to escape the clutch of her stare, I suppose I stumbled around rather badly.

She had no patience with my protestations. "Stammering does not become you," she said. Then, openly angry, "Did you honestly imagine I was so *obtusoso*—unspeakably proud, I would not know I was being made fun of?"

"But," I grumbled, "you looked pleased . . ."

"Do you know what it is to be raised as I have been, without sisters or brothers, in a place like Villalobos! To be imprisoned inside a mask imposed by the proprieties, to see your hopes die one by one and all your life—" She drew a deep breath, shuddering. Quietly she said, "It does not take much to please a *solterona*—a spinster, who has nothing but dead dreams to take to her bed."

The look of her saying so preposterous a thing to a man she had never seen before dampened my enthusiasm for touring the *hacienda.* There was small talk in the *sala*, the great main room of this feudal holding, over cakes and wine silently served by a *mozo* in cotton *pantalones.* I made my escape with as much celerity as conscience and the inquiring garrulity of my host would permit, but not before I'd been bound with the promise of returning for a tour of the place and dinner on a day to be determined no later than the following week.

Since night had overtaken me, Don Alfredo insisted on providing an escort, two stalwart *vaqueros* who evinced much interest in the subject of my horses. When we reached the river I was glad of their presence for, without it, in the dark I might have stumbled beyond my depth or bogged myself in quicksand. As it was, I scarcely even wet my boots.

Lamplight dimly shone from Dorrus' boar's nest. As I swung down by the porch he flung open the door. "Do you know," he demanded, "who that sonofabitch is?"

Thinking the fool was drunk, I said, "I don't even know what you're talking about."

"That high-pockets jasper with the scoopshovel jaw, one what claimed he was huntin' grouse! *Grouse!*" he snarled, glaring wildly and cursing. "That's the cold-hearted bastard shot Billy the Kid!"

VIII

I considered him over an interval of silence while my mind sized up several dark possibilities which, in view of his perturbation, obtruded themselves into the front of my thinking. "Pat Garrett?" I said.

"Who else!" he growled, glowering.

"But Ybarra said . . ."

"He says a pile of things besides his prayers! He ain't foolin' me! A guy kin git just as dead from a revenuer's bullet."

"The man collects customs."

"Hoo hoo!" Dorrus sneered. "Scalps is more like it! I kin tell you one thing. If that exterminatin' peckerneck comes pokin' around here—"

"Shirl," I said, "have you been mislaying Ybarra's cows?"

One arm came up to mop sweat streaked jowls. He flung irascibly about and stalked into the house. I followed him, shoving the door shut behind me. "You haven't answered my question."

"Helluva thing!"

I waited for him to turn. "If you've been tampering with his cattle . . ."

"You're bustin' a gut t' sell 'em—go ahead!" he snarled with a blustery look. "Sell the whole place if yer a goddam mind to!"

"That wouldn't solve anything."

In the sickly shine of the coal oil lamp his tobacco-stained snags gleamed like wolf fangs. "I never changed one mark!"

I looked at him, sighing. "There are other ways of doing it." What in blue blazes had I wedged myself into? "The penalty for mavericking in this state is hanging—had you thought about that?"

"They ain't caught nobody!" He glared defiantly. "That skillet of snakes brand of his ain't even registered this side of the river!" He swiped the sleeve across his jaws again. "They ain't," he grumbled, "got nothin' on me."

"For a man with clean skirts you make considerable commotion."

He scowled uncomfortably and scrubbed his hands along his pantslegs. "It's that goddam Garrett!" he shouted. "What's he care about proof! Look how he done poor Billy—"

"That was fifteen years ago."

"Drygulched the sonofabitch right in his bed!"

There was no good arguing with a man in Shirl's condition. Pat Garrett—if it was him, probably was here, like he said, trying out a new rifle. It just didn't seem reasonable he'd come clean down here all the way from El Paso to go poking around after Mexican cows. I peeled out of my coat. "Reckon I'll turn in. It's been a long day, and that slide I rode didn't help none."

• • •

I expect a man would go down in history—not to mention making a sizable fortune, if he could find some patentable way, through will, of putting himself to sleep when he wanted. Some means of drawing an impregnable curtain across nagging thoughts.

Well, I didn't have it; you may be sure of that. Nor did I toss or twist, except in my mind, but sleep wasn't in any rush to provide the release I craved from the things which beset me. Like gibbering phantoms they ringed my couch, jostling, bickering like ill-mannered children.

What if Shirl was right!

There was no one about when I awoke in mid-morning—not even the county seat barflies I'd hired who ought, at least, to have been waiting for their stipend.

Shirl had eaten and gone. Gone *where* I wondered with renewed disquiet as, shoving dirty dishes out of my way, I attempted to patch up some kind of a breakfast. He'd used the last of the cut wood, of course, there wasn't any kindling and the stove was cold as it could get in this temperature which must, I scowled, be well above a hundred.

With the sweat rolling out of me I got into my clothes and fed myself from an opened can of unappetizing peaches and three stale biscuits, burnt on the bottom and washed down with water from the near-emptied bucket. Just as I was finishing, the sound of a walking horse pulled me to the door.

Dorrus.

I called a good morning. Pulling up alongside the sagging porch he relieved his jaws of drowned tobacco, peered at me a spell and finally snorted. "I paid off them two hands. We've pushed that folly of yourn—all but the geldin's—on out t' Three Mile; it's the best graze we got, but if they ain't good rustlers yer goin' to hev t' buy feed."

"What about the geldings?"

Dorrus looked his disgust, spat again, said contemptuously, "What the hell good are eyes if you don't use 'em!"

Following his, I saw the five in a horse trap back of the day pen. I said after a moment, "What work have you laid out?"

"You got somethin' in mind?"

I had several things but, while looking them over, as Shirl sat waiting, a steeple-hatted rider loped up from the river with his mount dripping water, one of Ybarra's *vaqueros.*

Ignoring Shirl's ill concealed hostility the man informed me Don Alfredo would regard it as a favor if I could find the time to ride over this morning.

I rasped a hand across my chin. Though I had no wish to affront the old man, going again to the *hacienda* so soon on the heels of yesterday's visit did not appeal as either fitting or desirable with so many other more urgent matters clamoring for my attention. I wanted to get started with rebuilding. I wanted to get rid of those cattle for the money we could get out of them and to conserve what was left of the graze. While I was searching for some acceptable means of putting him off, the Mexican said apologetically, "I theenk, *señor*, it ees about the cattle . . ."

I caught the rush of an insucked breath, felt tension like cold rocks in my stomach while my glance, pulled narrow, searched and took hold of Ybarra's rider, endeavoring fiercely to keep his look off Shirl. "Tell Alfredo," I said, waving him away, "I'll be right over."

When the *vaquero* was gone I twisted round to face Shirl, wondering where all this was heading for.

The man was livid. "See!" he cried. "What'd I tell you! They're out t' nail—"

"You said they hadn't any proof."

"I—the guy's another Tom Horn! He'll do anythin' fer money!"

Shirl, of course, was talking through his hat. It was the guilt gnawing at him, panic fright. It had to be. The word, if Garrett had been that kind, would have been all over. I remembered the low, pleasant voice of the man, his modest demeanor, the cool mannered way he'd stepped into the breach when I'd childishly accused old Ybarra of trespassing. Garrett had twice been sheriff, a stock detective, he had ranched near Fort Stanton, had been a Texas Ranger. Shirl's charge was absurd.

But the fear bubbling in him, the wild roll of bugged eyes, sparked a sudden tingling hope that here might be something a man could use, with proper care, to remove the incubus of an unwanted partner. "All right," I said. "Stay close to the house till I find out what's up."

Motioning him down, I climbed into the saddle and rode off toward the ford, thinking there must be some way I could use the man's fright. I dredged up a number of things, crossing the river, but could not get around the papers that shyster was holding. If the man was hungry enough to be bought . . . My guts turned over and quivered with bitter insight. If he could, Shirl would buy him—probably already had!

IX

I disliked going over there. I was resentful of being summoned under what at best seemed a thinly veiled threat and I was, moreover, not a little annoyed at being impelled to arrive looking like something the dog had dragged in. I needed a shave and a bath, and was very much aware of it—not because of the girl but for the additional loss of face I should suffer in the eyes of that long-nosed old pelican who imagined, by God, he was the hub of the universe.

But I had, it appeared, no choice in the matter. My day might come, but if I was being called over there to talk about cattle it wasn't a thing that could very well be put off, not with Garrett involved and Dorrus with the wind up, prepared to burn powder at the drop of a hat.

Fussing and fuming, I passed through the great gate and down the huisach-lined lane, feeling the bite of the sun and the unstable character of this whole tricky business. I was becoming too tense, too aware of the disasters which might be lying in wait. I made a conscious effort to get rid of these forebodings, and saw ahead of me the white walls, the pink stone of the tower looming beyond through the branches.

Their leafy benevolence arched above me

greenly whispering in a lift of the breeze which served but to make me the more perceptive of the enormous stillness through which I rode. And so came, with cold misgiving, to the unguarded portal where I swung stiffly down to leave Shirl's horse on trailing reins.

With a growing reluctance I crossed the silent courtyard, seeing the scaly trunks of the pepper trees half hidden in the dancing froth of green foliage. The great house stood quiet, sun-drenched and alone, in its beds of lush semi-tropical flowers behind the chiseled stone of its entrance archway. The iron grilles were open, pressed back like the jaws of a baited trap, the tiny tinkles of sound struck up by my spurs swiftly lost in the hush.

I was shamed by the feeble timidity of my knock. Brusquely I struck the bossed mahogany again, anger giving my demand some authority. The near side opened to disclose the round stare of a white-garbed servant.

"Bancroft Benson," I gruffed. "I'm expected."

The man drew aside and I stepped into the *sala.* The door clanked shut. Mumbling something unintelligible the *mozo* fled into the dim silence of a bare door-flanked hall.

I was not kept long. Heralded by a rasp of squeaky bootsteps Don Alfredo came in, all smiles, hand extended. But, watching him suspiciously, I made out not to see. Ignoring my rudeness he clapped his hands, saying to the hatless servant who darted in, "See to the gentleman's horse. An armful of hay and—"

"Hold on!" I cried, "I can't stay!" and plunged on impatiently, "I was told you wanted to see me."

"Of course," Ybarra smiled, "but it will keep. Sit down, my friend. My poor house is yours. May I offer you some coffee? Perhaps some cakes and a glass of the *vino*? It was made in Hermosillo by—"

"I don't have the time." I scowled, feeling churlish. "What did you want of me? Your man seemed to . . ."

"Yes. Pablocito. *Muy impetuoso.* He worked on time in Del Norte and always now he is in the great hurry," Don Alfredo informed me with a tolerant chuckle. "Very *Americano*, Pablocito—but I digress. Forgive me. With your permission I should like to speak of those cattle, *señor*, the ones you bought with the little ranch."

"Yes?" I said.

"A thousand pardons, but if you still wish to sell them . . ." He must have noticed my surprise. "It is not, of course, that I have a great need, but if you haven't already arranged for their disposal I will be glad—since we are so closely situated—to take them off your hands." He smiled.

I considered him. "How much are you prepared to give?"

"How many do you count?"

I said, "I haven't made any count," and could have bitten my tongue.

But he did not appear to find anything unusual in my having bought the place without insisting on some sort of tally. "I am fairly well acquainted with what you have over there," he said pleasantly. "I will give you four thousand for the herd as it stands and round them up myself."

I was about to growl "Done!" when, with his smile widening out, he said, "Or race you for them, taking the cattle in any event but paying you five thousand for them if I should happen to lose. Speak up, friend. What do you say?"

"Race what?" I said, wary but excited.

"Did you not claim to be a breeder of horses? Anything you wish against my stallion Lágrimas *por tres estadios*—at three furlongs."

He must have done this before, I figured, to make such an offer with so much confidence. From the little he had seen he could hardly know anything about my horses. On that score, of course, we were in the same bind; but I had paid the Waggoners a fancy chunk of money to bolster my respect for the claims they had made. Had not their foreman solemnly put himself on record that every horse I'd bought was bred in speedy bloodlines? It could be a saving all around.

Still, I felt nervous. "And if I lose?"

"You get only three thousand for the cattle," he

smiled, "and I get in addition the horse you run against me."

I suppose it was the smile that finally tipped the scales. "All right!" I said, and grabbed up my hat.

But I was not to depart without seeing Linda.

She was gathering flowers and glanced up with bold eyes as I came from the house. She had the grace of a puma stepping into my path and, with that rainbow of posies, might have passed for a madonna. Except for the eyes and those magdalene lips.

"You are not staying for dinner?"

I'd heard enough about the upper-class customs of these people to suspect it was forbidden an unmarried female living at home to hold private conversation with an unattached man. I guess my apprehension showed. It fetched a low, husky laugh from that provocative youth. "Surely," she said, "you're not afraid of a *woman!*"

"But—"

"Are you then, as well, a thing of straw? Come, *señor*, let us see your manly daring." Slim, tiny waisted, she searched my face with her challenging stare. "*Norteamericanos* are notoriously progressive. Indeed, my Uncle Felix—he lives in Ciudad Juarez, calls them 'unrestrainably impetuous.' He is, of course, very old. Perhaps he speaks through his *sombrero.*" The petulant lips shaped a mocking smile.

"But, *señorita—*"

"Can you not say 'Linda'?"

I stabbed a worried look about.

She said, "A worm, I think. A squirming maggot." Her eyes matched the insolence.

The flush burned clean up into my hair, a heady anger clawing hard on its heels. For two cents, I thought . . . But it was no time for games. I felt her hand on my arm and tried to direct an appeal to her intelligence. "We're being most indiscreet."

"Pouf! You talk like my *duenna.* I am fed to the teeth with the pap of discretion!" Her eyes brightened imperiously. "Who's to hear . . ."

"There are servants . . ."

"Can you think one pays attention to them!" She tried to tighten her grip. I jerked away and stepped back, fiercely minded to shake her. The silly goose could get me in trouble with this madness. Spaniards are very strict with their women, particularly—

She must have picked up the thought. "You know, I could have you barred from this . . ." She looked suddenly pleased. "I could have you flogged!"

Was she out of her head?

At least she was not unaware of her power. Whatever she chose to say would be believed. It lay bright in her eyes, in the curve of her lips.

"I think, little mouse, you had better remember that."

X

She had given me something to think about, but the worries she stirred were overshadowed completely by the remarks of Shirl Dorrus when I gave him the gist of my talk with Ybarra.

His eyes looked about to come straight off his cheekbones. He couldn't have got redder if I had set out to strangle him. "You goddam swivel dude!" he yelled. "I ort t' take you apart an' throw the pieces away!"

I considered him uneasily. He looked more than half minded, I thought, to have a go at it. "If you're afraid of that race."

"Afraid of it!" His eyes were hot coals. "You ort t' be playin' with a string of spools! First place, by Gawd, you've put my neck in his hands! Top of that you—that fool hoss of his ain't never been beat!"

"He would hardly have offered to race if it had," I said with more assurance. "We've at least two horses and, maybe, three—"

Dorrus slammed his hat at the wall. "I should care about that?" His congested face turned livid with fury. "You peckerneck scissorbill! Can'tcher savvy it's the cattle that sonavabitch is after!"

"Cattle . . ." I said stupidly. "But we had already decided to get rid of—"

"Not t' *him,* you fool! What they cost don't matter. That race was chucked in t' purty it up fer you—Garrett's put him up t' this! He'll skin out ever' damn—"

"Skin?" I stared. Seemed to me if Shirl was headed for crazy he wouldn't have to camp out more than one night.

He gave me a black look. "Ain't you got nothin' under that hair? I tell you them bastards're after my scalp! If a brand's been teched up, surest way t' find out is t' cut off the piece. Underside of the hide'll tell straight off. Original brand always shows up strongest."

"But you said—"

"They'll find what they *want.* Make no doubt about that!"

He stomped out of the house.

I dropped into a chair, wondering what to do now. If Shirl was right about this, I couldn't honestly see how they could tie me in without Shirl's crew still was at it. I didn't know, of course, that they weren't. I'd have been inclined, however, to let them have Shirl if it wasn't for the papers that shyster was holding. I even wondered what kind of a partner *he'd* make.

The first storm hit the river that night, tearing out of the north with a wild roar of wind. Rain came down like a cartload of bullets. Thunder shook the house's streaming walls; lurid flashes of lightning, almost incessant, turned the night nearly bright as day.

We both got up—Rip van Winkle couldn't have slept through that. Shirl's curse-ridden gabble stayed the whole time on cattle. My own thoughts clung to the swollen river, wondering would it get on a fierce enough tear to gouge a new banco that would put Ybarra's holdings on our side of the boundary.

It was only a question of time—I knew that.

If it got the job done we could forget all this other stuff. The cattle wouldn't matter, nor the horses. I was getting a little worked up about those mares and colts. Texas Chief, who was the pappy of some of them, had been killed one night on the Waggoner ranch in weather like this; had got to running, they said, and wound up with his throat in the fork of a mesquite. It was a mort of money to have fly up the spout.

I went over to where Shirl stood glaring at the storm. "Fine weather for ducks," I grunted, and he plowed through his can of cusswords again.

It was coming down in sheets. Even with the lightning—and there was more than enough of that—you couldn't see Villalobos. More than half the time I couldn't even find the corrals.

I got to fretting about that fortune in horses. Catching up Shirl's yellow oilskin, I scrambled into it, fumbling with the buttons while I made for the door. His arm snaked out and spun me around. "Where you think yer off ter?"

He said, when I told him, "Ain't nobody goin' t' Three Mile in this!"

"Those geldings—" I said, and ran into his fist. I thought the damned roof had come down on my jaw. A snort and a shove slammed me into the chair. "Try usin' yer head instead of yer elbow! That's the river you hear—she's over her banks!"

Time stood still, but not Shirl Dorrus. The man was like a caged tiger. I sank back, jaw aching, to watch the ugly sight of him pacing, mouth stretched tight across the humps of his teeth, a maddening example of the one track mind. All he could think about was those cows. "No tellin' where they've got ter," he muttered. "Goddam spiks'll hev their work cut out. One good thing, they won't be combin' them brakes in no handful of hours!"

I stared distastefully at the tramp of his shadow. "Give you time enough to run."

He came around with a curse, stiffening, peering. The whole look of him hardened. "So that's what yer up ter!" He loosed a bark of a laugh. "Yer'll hev t' do better'n that, laddybuck, if yer figgerin' t' git yerself shut of Shirl Dorrus!" His head came back out on his neck. Like a vulture he looked with those beady black eyes shining in the lamp glow. "I ort t' break yer schemin' goddam neck!"

He went back to his tramping.

The rain beat down. The thunder moved grumbling off through the hills and still his shadow blackly wheeled to and fro with the crazy precision of an out-of-whack pendulum. I closed my eyes, listening to the raucous song of the river.

I must have dozed. When I next looked around the lamp still burned but I was alone in the place and the gray light of day was frothed across the windows. Shirl's slicker rattled against the chair when I got up stiffly, crackling about my legs when I moved to yank open the door. There was nothing to see but thick white fog. The only sound was the roar of the river.

I scraped my face and threw together some food. Not much sense going out into that. I did wonder if we had any rideable horses left. Probably find them all drowned or hung up in the brush. Somewhat more cheerfully I thought of Ybarra. Would this be the day I'd been planning and waiting for?

I was just sitting down to my second cup of coffee when Shirl, all beaded with dampness, came in. He had mud on his boots halfway up to his knees.

"Can't see three yards in that goddam soup. Take a week t' dry out—gumbo all over. Gumbo an' frogs!" He looked at me sourly. "Yer geldin's is gone. Trap's got three foot of water standin' in it."

I couldn't help sighing. "At least it will bring up the grass. You look at the river?"

"Still on rampage," he grumbled, starting off.

"Did you *look* at it?" I said, and he came half around, peering.

"What would I wanna . . ." He stopped, stare sharpening. "What's the river got t' do with it?"

I managed, I think, to dredge up a look of puzzlement, but he had plainly got his teeth in something and, bulldog like, was determined to hang on. I said with concern, "Do you have these spells often?"

He peered at me a while and then, grin ugly, went back outside.

It wouldn't do him any good. I realized now that if the river had moved he couldn't have helped but notice, living here like he had, God knew how many years, but he was proving a lot sharper than I had given him credit for. And a sight more dangerous.

I was going to have to watch my tongue. I even wondered with some disquiet if I might not better start packing a pistol. But the lack of arms was my best defense and I had sense enough to see this.

"Burn through by noon," he said, coming back. "But there won't be nobody crossin' that water fer another couple days, way it's runnin' right now." He pulled off his wet shirt and, with his head to one side, peered around at me shrewdly. "That what yer wanted t' know?"

If it would keep him quiet I was willing he should think so. "I did sort of promise to take dinner over there."

"Hard lines," he said, nodding, but continuing to weigh me. "Fer a gent as can't stand bein' cooped with a woman you ain't doin' half bad. Why'n't yer fergit this fal-de-rah with the hosses an' go ahead an' marry her?"

"Now, look." I growled.

He wasn't pretending to listen. "That way," he said soft as spider feet, not smiling, "should somethin' happen to her daddy, we'd be already in. Waitin' an' worryin's no good fer a man. You think about it, sport." He got into a dry shirt and reached his slicker off the peg where I'd hung it. His pseudo good humor peeled away like old skin. "When I git back you better hev a answer."

XI

He was right about the fog, but proved considerably unreliable on several other counts. Short of noon while I was deep in the problem of what to do about him the sun broke through, bright as a gold piece fresh from Frisco. Half an hour later, opening some tinned grub without having come to any firm decision, I was brought to the porch by a hail from outside to stare, drop jawed, at Ybarra's man Pablo.

The roar and rumble of the river was nearly deafening out here. From that churning flood of tumbling waters I passed disbelieving eyes over mud plastered legs that had no horse between them; and so, incredibly, looked into that grinning face. *Muy impetuoso* his master had called this fellow, but it certainly had not prepared me to face a walking miracle.

"*Buenos dias, señor*," he chuckled, hugely pleased with my astonishment.

"Where's your horse?" I said, not sure I wasn't dreaming this.

"*No caballo, señor.* We 'ave build the boat."

I looked again at that wild stretch of water. "Come in," I grumbled, "I'll fix you a drink . . . I think I better have one myself."

I poured two half tumblers and we tossed them

off. “So you built a boat. Just like that. Couldn’t wait, I suppose, until the river went down?”

“But no, *señor.* The *patrón* ees t’row *baile*—w’at you call beeg ‘weendeeg’ tonight. For the Don Patricio. You are particular eenvite—the Señor Dorrus, likewise. *Mirar*!” He drew a folded paper from his shirt.

Opening it, I read:

> *Mr. Benson*
>
> *In the morning Mr. Garett is leaving for Del Norte. Tonight we are having a few people in—a kind of party. I was asked particularly to invite yourself and Mr. Dorrus.*
>
> *Linda Ybarra.*
>
> *Please come. Pablo has instructions to bring you in the boat.*

I read it again, and was not reassured. It appeared, on the face of it, innocuous enough, but I sensed disquieting implications. There was an urgency here that raised my hackles. Nothing had been said yesterday about Garrett leaving; no party had been mentioned. Yet Pablo “has instructions” . . . Pablo the impetuous who had worked in Del Norte. Suddenly we were wanted on the other side of the Line. Badly enough that a boat had been built to get word across and fetch us. Piloted by an ignorant peon and hand crafted . . . from what? A boat that, at best, could be hardly more than a chip in a millrace.

I refilled Pablo's glass and, chewing my lip, peered again out across that tumbling, turgid, debris-laden river that looked to be at least three times its normal width. How in God's name had the fool ever made it!

I poured another for Bancroft Benson. It had the teeth of a beaver, the scald capacity of boiling lava, and never got near the chill in my bones. If Ybarra's aim was to safely get rid of us, he could hardly have hit on a more practical solution.

But *was* that his aim?

Was he seeking to be rid of us, or only to comfort us at a time and in a place where every advantage would lie solidly behind him? And, if so, to what purpose? Would he be so incensed over a handful of cattle?

Unsure, confused, and considerably disturbed, I turned to find in the doorway behind Ybarra's man the whiskered scowling shape of Dorrus with a white knuckled fist wrapped about the butt of his pistol.

Pablo, rolling around in his tracks, went breathlessly still, losing much of his tan. Shirl's gun was not drawn but, if looks stood for anything, there was scarcely one shout between that Mex and eternity.

You could see the shine of sweat on his cheeks.

Shirl jabbed out a hand. “Lemme lookit that thing.”

“We don’t know she wrote it,” I said, passing it over.

Dorrus read it, crumpled it and flung it away from him. His eyes burned at Pablo. “Git yer chin ag’in’ that wall!”

“Let’s not do anything hasty,” I said.

All it got out of Shirl was a look of contempt. Pablo, eyes rolling, sent a fearful look at me before, crossing himself with a kind of stoic fatalism, he bellied the wall.

I drew a deep breath. It was Shirl did the talking. After slapping the Mexican over for weapons he ordered him inside and kicked the door shut. A child could have sensed the fury that had hold of him. With his chopped off ears and broken snags, and the scraggly beard that swirled over his jowls, he was a pretty unlovely sight, I can tell you. “What kind of deal hev you ribbed up with them bastards?”

My lungs filled with protest. The words stuck in my throat. The malevolence in those mean little eyes was too real and too near.

I knew then what kind of mad dog I’d teamed up with. The frenzy of violence boiling back of that stare left no doubt of his proclivities. The man was a killer with no more conscience than a prodded snake.

It wasn’t courage that pulled words out of me.

"If you believe that," I growled, "we better tear up those papers."

"What else kin I think!"

"Think?" I said. "Don't make me laugh!" and, in sheer desperation, I slammed around to stalk off, never imagining he'd let me. Nor did he. Spun about, I stood gingerly flexing my arm, somewhat astonished he hadn't tore it clean off.

He looked ugly enough. "That ain't even a patch to what yer kin look fer if I ever find reason t' really take holt. Now start singin'."

"I don't know what they're—"

"Never mind *them!* I wasn't borned yestiday! You won't ketch me goin' over that river—an' if you got half the sense Gawd give a blind gopher, you won't."

"But I've *got* to!"

"Why?"

I glared in frustration. Put like that I couldn't make it look sensible. All the half hatched reasons floating round in my head became insubstantial as a flutter of cobwebs. I couldn't imagine him swallowing such hogwash. "It's just something I've got to do, is all."

The hateful grin crawled over his mouth. "I'll buy that, sport." The look in his stare brought a burn to my face. "Reckoned she'd git t' you, give 'er time."

I slammed into the house, too furious to answer.

• • •

Ignoring Ybarra's *vaquero* I stripped to the buff, dipping and scrubbing from the bucket at the sink until my hide, from that yellow soap, felt as though I'd used a piece of malapie on it. I was wild enough to go up in smoke.

I grabbed clean clothes from my bag and flung into them, still going over that scene with Shirl. Hauling open the door I heaved out my slops. I glared about without discovering him and, back inside, got into my coat and bitterly snatched up my hat. "Let's go!" I growled, brusquely motioning Ybarra's peon ahead of me.

It was strictly a matter of diplomacy, of course—the girl had nothing to do with it. Shirl wouldn't believe Pat Garrett was leaving but if he was, it could change a whole lot of things. And that party now . . . good chance to size up Ybarra's friends and learn what odds we were like to be up against when we set out to take the place away from him. If they were going to prove troublesome, now was the time to be finding out.

Nor was Shirl alone in his distrust of that old man. Cold quivers were scrabbling all through the insides of me, my nerves taut as fiddle strings—but what choice did I have? There were things we needed to know, besides Garrett . . . and the godawful prospect of bucking that river was one more hitch those Ybarras had put on me. They must have known we'd be suspicious. It was like I was being dared to come over there!

Something else popped into my head to show the guile of him. The way I'd been cozened into agreeing to that race. The only thing I had that a man could get onto was Tom Rock, a stallion, and even if I could get him away from the mares who would I put on him?

When I saw the "boat" I pretty near threw in my hand. Three logs, cross-spiked at both ends, a pair of beer kegs for seats secured with rope lashings, two up-ended spurs fixed amidship for rowlocks. "God save us!" I said, with a shudder of revulsion.

XII

We made it.

Don't ask me how. There are times, even now, I break out in cold sweat, gripped by some fragmentary glimpse of forgotten terrors, nightmare impressions too awful to grasp or pin down with bald words.

What words can recapture the bullet speed of wild water, the strangling impact, breathless agonies or ghastly horror of such an experience? Can words measure the pulse pound of the human heart?

We got across, spewed out upon a muddy shore a long three miles below the ford when our thing of logs tore apart beneath us and was instantly gone in that churning roar.

How long I lay, gasping and flapping like some gaffed fish, I've no idea. In spite of the mauling I could probably have moved had I not been so damned scared to try. After that I was too filled with the wonder of my deliverance to have much thought for anything else. Then, piece by piece, I went over myself, seeking out the scrapes and ugly bruises. When at last I lurched from the suck of the mud to go stumbling about in a hunt for Pablo it was to find the poor devil draped across the wreckage of a shoved-in keg. I could see right away he wasn't going to get up.

The fiend who invented cowpuncher boots should have trudged that quagmire trek with me through slashes of cedar and white-eyed, bellering, berserk cattle. You'd be amazed what a man can do when he has to. I astonished myself.

In my condition a few days ago I would probably have been back there with dead Pablo, or too stupid with abuse to care if school kept or not. But rage, I was discovering, could be a mighty stimulant, a powerful incentive, inexorably demanding as the pull of raw gold.

That I was here under false pretenses to defraud an old fool, to grab for my own what should be rightfully that girl's, never entered my head. *I* was the injured one. Every sorry turn my fate had taken could be tracked to the door of Don Alfredo.

That crazy old man! God, how I blazed! Without this fury I probably never would have made it.

When the tiles and rain-damp walls of Villalobos finally showed through the never-ending cedar I was stumbling along like a tangle-footed runk, as near to being off my rocker as a man is likely to come without getting there. I remember being helped into the house through a phalanx of staring faces, of collapsing onto some darkening sofa—and the gabble of voices.

The next I recall is of waking up staring at a whitewashed ceiling of ocotillo wands laid over adzed timbers. Whitened burlap-covered walls were bright with sunlight, bare except for the Jesus on a cross and a home-built chair occupied at the moment by the buxom, shawl-draped presence of Linda's dumpy *dueña*, one Marisca by name. The dark face spread in a flash of white teeth when she discovered my open eyes.

"The *patrón* . . ." I cried, starting up, only to subside with an astonished grimace as the room swam around me in dizzying waves. "The *baile—*" I gasped; and felt the coolness of her hand pressing me back against the sheets.

Digging back into my impressions I seem to have been conscious of much activity revolving about me without being able to pull anything into focus. I suppose I was fed and pretty generally looked after. All I recall with any clarity was the hook-nosed face of Ybarra standing over me, smiling with indulgence when, somewhat petulantly no doubt, I demanded to be told what he'd done with my clothes.

It must have sounded pretty childish. I can't bring back his words or look, except I'm sure he didn't laugh. All I can manage to bring out of it now is a feeling of sadness, a kind of vast patience, imperturbable as the land itself. I was determined, I remember, not to miss the big doings for which I had come at such risk to Villalobos.

"The *baile*, my friend," Ybarra said with a sigh, "was eight nights past."

I suppose I gaped like a ninny. Don Alfredo, clapping his hands, summoned a *mozo*, mumbling something in Spanish which sent the man off. He returned with a glass-and-tin Mexican mirror which, at Ybarra's nod, he held up in front of me. I stared at the whiskered wild-eyed look of the hollow-cheeked stranger peering back at me, one side of his head a white swath of bandaging.

"That was bad, but you'll be all right now," Ybarra assured me, waving the man away. "You must compose yourself and—"

"Where's Garrett!" I cried, pushing up on one elbow, all the problems I had fetched here coming back to clutch and prod me.

The man had gone back to Paso del Norte, the old man replied, considering me with what I took for a sharpened interest. And I was not to worry about my ranch; everything was being looked after with "*mucho gusto*" by my *segundo*—almost, Ybarra smiled, as though the place were still his own.

The next day I was bathed and shaved and, in the afternoon, allowed to sit up against a cartload of stuffed-in pillows. Linda came by—with Marisca, of course, and visited a while, giving me such news as she deemed agreeable. Roundup, she said, of the Running Bee cattle was nearing completion. Dorrus had brought in someone to work with the horses; the *adobes* for my new house were all made and stacked and, tomorrow, Don Alfredo was sending over a crew of peons to get the walls up, and the furnishing she had picked out and ordered on my behalf—through her father, of course—would no doubt be along by the time it was finished.

When I collected enough breath to make myself heard—and it took some doing in the face of all that, without stopping to reflect how ungrateful it might sound I demanded to be told whose idea it had been to run up these bills without asking my permission.

She looked a little surprised. "But they're all things you said yourself you were going to do."

"Not at one fell swoop!" I suppose I looked pretty much put out, because she said as though it left no ground for complaints. "My father's *vaqueros* have been gathering the cattle; there's no cost to you there. Our people made the *adobes*, and—"

"All right," I growled, it having suddenly occurred to me how niggardly and childish my attitude must seem in a man who had set himself up to be at least a *rico* if not a member of the *gente*. The ground was quivering under me. The whole facade of my pretended great wealth was being threatened by this carping.

People living glass houses could not afford to throw rocks. I had to get that thoughtful look off her face, and took the only line that appeared to hold any hope. "It's not the cost," I grumbled, twisting up a parched smile. "It's just that . . ."

"Yes?"

I said, grinding my teeth, "When a man's been as busy as I have, Linda, piling up a stake and trying to stay on top of it . . . What I'm trying to say is, he ain't had much time to pretty up his words."

I could feel the heat pounding into my cheeks. Her arrested scrutiny sent me clumsily on. "It's not," I said, "that I don't appreciate the way you and your dad have pitched in to help me. It's just that . . . Well, dang it, a man likes to . . . to surprise a woman."

"I think you are becoming delirious," she said and, turning her head, hurried out of the room, but not before I'd caught the change in her eyes.

The *dueña*, Marisca, as she waddled past to follow, gave me one sharp look and said in completely comprehensible English: "Have a care what kind of games you play, gringo."

XIII

During the next couple of weeks I was probably the only fellow on the Running Bee who could find time enough to draw a full breath. The water went down. The new corrals were up, set and tamped, lashed Mexican-style with strips of stinking rawhide by the two Dorrus hands I'd never got around to sacking.

With all the cows gone—driven off across the river by Ybarra's *vaqueros*—we needed the two barflies like a squirrel needs a piccolo; yet every time I fetched up the subject Shirl with his stratagems put me off. Last time I'd tried he'd come around, cursing, to shape his face into mine.

"They're staying—is that plain?"

You could see the black temper boiling back of his stare. I guess my own was pretty ragged. He said, easing off a little, "Chrissake, Bancroft! How do we know what that bastard is up to? He's got them cows—you got nothin' but his word he'll ever pay you one nickel. 'Fore we git done with this fool-crazy play we're like t' need ever' damn gun we kin git!"

Didn't seem much point getting banged up about it. Cost of two hands and their grub wouldn't break us and really these rannies, against the tall look of more discernible worries, lifted scarcely a smudge. I supposed I could afford to let Shirl have his way in this.

Besides, there was Ybarra. He might think it odd—even downright peculiar—if I was to send the whole crew packing. "All right," I grumbled with a shrug, and walked off.

Still, it rankled. And what Shirl had said about Ybarra scraped, too. Nor did it ease me any that, at least up to this point, the most of Shirl's alarms had proved without substance. There was generally a first time for just about everything. Supposing Ybarra did try to wriggle out of it!

Could he be compelled to pay? He already had the cattle. The law couldn't help—not with them where they were now, across the river. If for once Shirl was right I didn't have a leg to stand on. I would look pretty silly if, after that race that was to decide which price he paid, the hook-nosed old pirate sat tight and paid me nothing.

The new house was up, finished and furnished with the truck picked out by Linda and which, of course, I'd had to pay for. This had put me into debt at the bank. Every time I looked at the stuff I burned anew. A lot of spindly gingerbread crap, and the only chance I could see of paying out was to win that race I'd been talked into by her father. The more I heard about that damned racer Lágrimas the more unlikely it appeared that I would do it.

Sometimes, when I got off to where without interruption I could look the whole deal over, I could almost have sworn I was the deliberate picked-out victim of some devilish conspiracy. Even the blasted weather was against me. This heat was ferocious. Since that one useless storm we'd had nothing but sun and blistering winds. The three inches of grass that had grown in its wake was beginning already to curl up with wilt.

I was not at all happy with the galoot Shirl had got to work the kinks out of those unbroken Waggoner horses. Sancho Daguerrias had all the earmarks of what is called in the East a "cheap racetrack tout." His flashy cap and plaid jacket would have appeared more at home around Saratoga. He didn't look to be able to make ninety pounds wet, and seemed devious and shifty as a sackful of snakes.

"Fer Chrissake!" Shirl snarled. "You buyin' talent or looks? Fer five bucks a day you reckon t' git Lillian Russell? This guy's been a jock, right up in the big time—N'Orleans, Narraganset—you name it, he's been there! Ain't a trick in the book this feller don't know."

"All I want is an honest ride."

Shirl said to me, scowling, "You better take him an' like it. You got a hoss an' two thousand at stake in this go-round!"

I buttoned my lip, but I was a long way from

liking it, and the longer I watched the more steamed up I got. There wasn't much doubt but what the man knew his job. He spent the whole first morning of what time I was out there just squatting in the shade, staring at the geldings Dorrus' hands had run in. Every little while he'd have the boys stir them up. After grub we went back and one of the hands roped Granite for him, moving the big gray around on a halter.

I walked up to them, curiosity getting the best of me. "This the one you're going to ride against Lágrimas?"

"Dunno," he mumbled, considering me slyly. "You got something better?"

"You're supposed to be the 'expert' around here."

He studied me a while, presently nodding. "What I figured." He looked again at the gelding. "How's this plug bred?"

"That's Granite," I told him, bearing down on my temper. "Second generation Traveler. Sired by Texas Chief, that was bred by the Shelys, out of the slip-shouldered bay by Gardner's blue roan."

"Yeah?" He didn't appear much impressed. Up on his feet again, head to one side, he stepped back for a prolonged three-quarters view. "We goin' to run from a flag or will it be lap an' tap?"

"Does it make any difference?"

Daguerrias looked pained. He peered into the

sky, swallowed a couple of times, considered me again, told the hand with the halter shank to walk the horse through some more figure eights. "Man's got his work cut out, tyin' into a hot-blood with stuff like this. You should of gone for a quarter."

"How do you mean?"

"At the quarter these hides would probably shake up some dust. But six-sixty . . . I dunno. They look pretty short."

It was all Greek to me. His little shifty eyes must have taken that in. He said with a sigh, "I'm goin' to give it to you straight. If you got any choice make it lap an' tap."

"What's that?" I said.

The way he looked I might have asked where the moon was. "It's a method of starting," he finally declared. "You got a startin' line—see? But the hides don't go until they both hit the line headed the same way an' lapped. Is this thing goin' to be timed?"

"We haven't discussed the arrangements."

"Then you better get at it. I can't do you no good till I know what we're up against." Behind that old-young sharp little dried-apple face he stood scowling for a bit, chewing something over. "Better for us if you could make it ask an' answer. Most of the sprints he's been in at Juarez that stud has took off from a forty-foot score, the flag not droppin' till they crossed the line.

Hard boot style," he said, like that explained everything.

If I'd got to appear ignorant, I'd sooner look foolish in front of him than Ybarra. "What do you mean, ask and answer?"

Whatever this shrimp had been minded to say he apparently swallowed. Though he looked disgusted, he said mildly enough, "That's where the riders start themselves. Comin' up to the line they take turns askin' *'Ready?'* Whenever the asked guy likes it he yells *'Go!'* and they're off. Takes a cool head—"

"Sounds tricky," I said, considering him dubiously.

"Better have your mind washed out with soap."

When he discovered I wasn't answering his grin he said, sounding caustic; "If you don't want to win—"

"I want to win, all right. But I sure hadn't figured on having to cheat."

"Who said anything about cheatin'? You're goin' up against a papered horse, mister, a high-strung fidgety bolt of blue lightning! At six hundred yards this hide here of yours is going to be huntin' a hole to fall into. Cheatin'! You call it cheatin' to try to give yourself a chance?"

"If you think so poorly of Granite," I said, graveled, "what's the matter with running that stud of mine at him?"

Daguerrias threw up his hands.

"His pappy," I growled, "beat Pan Zareta twice."

"Then he sure as hell wasn't loafin' around with no bunch of mares! This matched race stuff can be murder, mister. Some of these jocks—"

I waved it away.

The only jock worrying me was *him.* If this seems paradoxical I suppose it was because, from the very inception of this rags-to-riches venture, I had been too engrossed with the mechanics of my purpose to take a square look at what I'd set out to do. In the finders-keepers way of a kid I looked on Villalobos as legitimate prey, a prize to be snatched by the first one to see it.

The race I regarded as a sporting proposition, a calculated risk, the very nature of its challenge inclining me to view with something tantamount to horror the exposure of myself before Ybarra as a cheat. I would almost rather lose the race.

I tell you, goddamit, I felt actually ill.

Considering the man with a sick repugnance, I beckoned him off to one side out of hearing. "Put a straight ride on him and, whatever Dorrus promised, I'll double it—understand?"

Did his lip curl a little? At any rate, he nodded.

I turned away, took one step and, nervously, swung back. My stomach crawled with loathing. "If you win," I said, "you get a hundred dollar bonus."

• • •

Shirl met me at the door. He had never looked so rankly suspicious, or more viciously determined. One arm lashed out to fist my shirt, his other hand dug a gun in my belly. "You wouldn't be crossin' me would you, sport?"

His grip made it almost impossible to speak. His mean little eyes never left my face. "I been watchin' you out there! What kinda deal did you make with that twirp?"

I'll admit I was frightened. I gulped out the truth. He glared, grip tightening. "You expect me t' swaller that?"

Like some berserk ape, one handed, cheeks darkening, he hauled me up till my feet wouldn't touch. The crazy way he shook me I figured everything inside would come loose. With a snarl he slammed me into a porch post.

I saw the gun coming up. "Shirl," I cried, desperate, "for God's sake, ask him!"

He stood winklessly still for what seemed an eternity, pinning me with the wild shine of his eyes. I thought to Christ my spine had been sprung. I scarcely dared breathe.

Then he said, stepping back, "Tell me now how we go about takin' Villalobos."

XIV

It had not been my intention to go into this with Shirl until the time came to seize the place. It was not in my best interest to uncover so early the holecard of what I'd found out about bancos, to explain how the river was going to drop Villalobos right into our laps. But the look of him held a compelling persuasiveness.

I talked like a man with diarrhea of the jawbone and his scowl grew uglier with every word that tumbled out.

How could he appear so bitterly affronted? I cried, "Don't you believe me?"

Whatever I had looked for, it certainly wasn't this. Ramming the pistol into his holster the sonofabitch stomped off without a word.

To hell with him, I snarled; and, getting a mount from the day pen, set off for the *hacienda.* There seemed nothing right then more important to me than getting the conditions of that race straightened out.

But, as I rode, the resentments he'd fed with this high-handed treatment broke through the flimsy defense I'd thrown up to curl like flames around the personal estimate of self I had cherished. This tottering image began to tarnish and wrinkle in the acid memory of the fright I'd been given, child-helpless in that terrible grip.

I saw in these shambles some things clearer, but the brightest thing inside me was anger. Like a wind it sang in widening clamor; and so I came to the river and through the sunset shine of it discovered, dark above the far shore, a solitary horseman, motionless as rock. As I peered, one arm moved in a beckoning gesture.

I kneed my mount into the crimson water. It found the ford and not until we were halfway across did I realize the beckoner was Linda. I was minded to turn back but went stubbornly on; telling her would be no harder than appearing as a supplicant before her long-nosed sire.

Splashing out of the river I drew rein beside her. She was exotically appareled in the Spanish manner and gave the impression of being pleased to see me. "Are you visiting Villalobos?" she asked, smiling prettily.

Finding her red mouth strangely exciting, I said gruffly, "An errand only," but was quick to note how well she looked. "I was coming about the race," I told her. "If Don Alfredo could find it agreeable it would suit me to break from a flat-footed score."

She raised her heavy brows but, still smiling, said, "As the challenged party it is your privilege, *señor.* Impose whatever conditions will most advantage you. My father would think you a fool if you did not."

“Then tell him,” I said, “we’ll start Texas fashion. Two days after tomorrow.”

She considered me curiously. “Is this the animal you will ride against Lágrimas?”

I glanced down, a bit startled—not so much at the open scorn of her question as at the discovery of finding a Waggoner mare under me. Dredging up a smile of my own, I said, “Who can tell where the owl will cry or what fool thing a crazy gringo will do?” and, sweeping off my hat in the father of flourishes, put the mare back into the river.

There was no evidence of Shirl when I rode up to the house, nor inside could I find any trace of the paper on which Waggoner’s foreman had put down particulars of the horses I’d bought. But I recalled well enough what he had told me about them; except for the stallion, only the geldings had been ridden.

It seemed my partner had managed to keep busy while I had been laid up from my bout with the river. Back outside I stood thoughtfully looking over the mare I had just ridden across the river. This was Cajun Queen, the club-footed mare, sired by Tom Glover, a big name in polo.

My head swirled with questions. Obviously someone had put in some time with her. She was shod. A bar had been put across the heel of her bad hoof. I pulled off my saddle and put her back where I’d found her in the new day pen they had built for the geldings. Why had she been broken? Toward what end was she being kept up?

I had breakfast with Shirl, neither one of us saying much. When he stepped out I went with him. When he took the rope down off his saddle, starting around toward the pen's gate, I tagged along.

He twisted around. "Somethin' on yer mind?"

"I guess it can wait."

Snorting, he bent and crawled through the poles. I watched the shifting horses melt away from his advance, saw the rope snake out and catch the mare's club foot. She stopped in her tracks, waiting for him, trembling.

His glance cut around, I guess to see how I was taking it. His two cowhands came up with Daguerrias as he led her out. The horsemaster sent in a hand for the gray. Granite saw him coming and slid away behind the bunch. Dust rose from their milling hoofs and the first loop dropped off the back of a dun, but when the rope sang again the big gray ran into it. By this time Shirl, saddled up, was riding off.

The man on the rope brought Granite out. While the other hired hand was putting up the bars I said to Daguerrias, "You have anything to do with gentling that mare?"

"I broke her out."

"On whose orders?"

He studied me from the corners of his eyes,

told the man holding Granite to take him over to the forge. He was fixing to go after them when I put out a hand. "Tomorrow," I said, "put racing plates on her."

He shifted uncomfortably. "Shirl's satisfied."

"Shirl isn't paying the bills around here."

He couldn't seem to find any answer to that. Looking more squirmy, he finally said in a kind of whine, "What do you wanta go doin' that for?"

"Because," I said, "I've an idea she's fast. I think she was your pick. Then, when Shirl took her away from you—"

"I never . . ." His eyes slid away and he licked at cracked lips.

"It's obvious enough." I grinned at him bleakly. "We've all got our pet devils, you know. Shirl intends to be able to run if he has to. Cheer up," I said to his look of dismay. "The sky hasn't fallen. Shirl's my worry. The only pay you'd get out of him is a bullet."

XV

Advising others is both easy and pleasant when whatever they do will take no skin off one's nose, but I was not quite the fatuous ass you might think. I'd not the slightest intention of reposing great trust in him, nor had it slipped my mind the most likely target for Shirl's trigger finger was the hide and hocks of Bancroft Benson.

At earliest opportunity Daguerrias, probably, would report my words, and whatever he deemed my most obvious intentions. They could not, however, be sure of their assumptions.

This uncertainty, and any tensions if bred, would compel Shirl to ready at least one alternate series of moves. There was bound to be some confusion about it and any preoccupation at all, coupled to the remembered threat of signed papers, should keep Dorrus off my back for a while.

Had that been all I might have seen where to jump, but there was also Ybarra and that rabble of peons like a rock hanging over me . . . the words of Marisca. Games and gringos. Nor was Linda ever very far from the rumpled contour of my apprehensive thoughts.

I was like a man trying to cross a pond on the swaying shimmer of winter's first ice, conscious of black depths, tense with the horror of that awful cold.

Shirl stayed out of my sight the rest of that day. He was not in the house when I got scowlingly up at first light to throw together and gulp whatever came handiest, washed down with gall-strong, warmed-over java.

Through the window, as I stood up, I observed Daguerrias bound for the pens with Shirl's two brush poppers coughing and hawking as they stumped along after him.

All of the cold wasn't in my bones. There was enough in the air that you could see their breath.

I got into a brush jacket, clapped on a hat, stood fast at the window until the mare was led out. They were prepared, anyway, to make a show of following orders.

One more time I re-examined my position and, with a shivery disquiet, dug a short-barreled .38 revolver from my duffle, stood bodefully eyeing it before, more nervous still, I thrust it angrily away and quit the house.

Daguerrias, when I came up, was squatted frowningly alongside the mare with one lifted hoof in the palm of his hand. This he presently eased to the ground and, with a figuring look in his half-shut eyes, ducked under her head to catch up the other. I could have been clear at the back end of China for all the notice that monkey face paid me.

"Well?" I said gruffly.

He presently let go of the hoof and stood up. "Take her over to the forge," he bade Shirl's hands, and looked around at me, grunting. "It's your choice, your money. Better think this over. The gray might not have as much early foot, an' he'll probably run short, but what he's got you'll get every bit of it. You don't know what this damn sow will do."

That wasn't all I didn't know.

Through the confusions besetting me I seemed to hear again the scorn of Linda's voice. Had she put the question that way as a dare . . . a kind of challenge? Did she *want* Lágrimas beaten?

I peered irritably at the man. I didn't know he'd been bribed to lose this race. How could it advantage Shirl? Was it pure bullheadedness that made me distrust him? I said, "We're going to run Queen, so make up your mind to it."

His furtive stare slid away in a grunt of disgust. "Like I said, it's your choice. They're your hides, mister." He wheeled back to say bitterly, "I'm not denyin' her gifts. She's got a world of power in that squatty hind end. She'll come off that score like a bat out of Carlsbad, and that'll be it. If she goes ten jumps, by God, I'll—"

"Let's get down to facts. I helped fetch these horses out from the railroad."

"That wasn't no race. She's quick an' she's willin', but have you looked at her feet—really looked at them? The walls of that hoof ain't no thicker than paper. You know what'll happen when she turns on the power? She'll throw that shoe in the first three jumps!"

"Racing plates?"

"You can't keep plates on her. She spreads them."

Suddenly grinning, I said, "So we'll run her barefoot," and started back to the house while his mouth was still open.

Shirl's burly shape blocked the door. The black ugliness in him showed plain through the slits of his half shut eyes. He stepped aside finally and I went on in with the baleful feel of him thick enough cut; and so came, greased with sweat, to a frozen legged stop, incredulously staring at Linda Ybarra.

I said, like a fool, "I didn't notice your horse . . ." and the brittle quiet, the stick-like stiffness of her coupled to the remembrance of Shirl's look and placement, began to get through to me. Her face was as white as olive skin can get.

The twisted waist, the dangling ends of torn sleeve, exploded across my reeling vision. Only barely was I able to move in time as, swaying, eyes rolling, she fell whimpering into my convulsive embrace.

God alone knows what we felt or thought in the roar and chaos of that traumatic interval. I expect

I said some pretty ridiculous things—I remember the clean heady smell of her hair, the stifled sobs that shook the wondrous soft feel of her pressed as she was so fearfully against me.

Somewhere I found the strength to break free. Shaking, panting, half out of my mind, I left my strewn duffle with the gun in my fist.

"No!" she cried. "Oh—no!"

I was halfway to the door, deaf with the clamor of outraged needs, when her hands caught and held me with the terror of her fright. Like a clutch of steel they forced me around to face the scared wet shine of her eyes.

I said, "Linda, I've got—" and could feel her grip tighten.

"No! He didn't . . . I'm not hurt—let him go." She brushed a hand across my cheeks, as a blind person might, as though to etch their shape deep in memory. Suddenly she was crying, and I pulled her to me, unable to speak.

XVI

"Is she ready?" I said to Daguerrias next morning.

You couldn't have sworn he really snorted, though the glance I got he might just as well have. "Ready as she'll ever be," he grumpily sneered with a shrug that disclaimed any part in such foolishness. He would have liked to say more, but a narrowing look at my face did not encourage it.

"Where's Shirl?" I asked, and he managed to shrug out from under that, also. I hadn't seen Dorrus since that business with Linda and, now that I'd had time to simmer down a little, I'd have been just as well suited if I never did again.

It was a muggy day, sticky and close beneath an overcast sky, as if a storm was working up back of the rimrocks. It wouldn't have surprised me to have heard thunder rumble. "You got those cowboy shoes off her yet?"

He stared. "You ain't serious?"

"Where is she? Who's with her?"

He blew out his cheeks. "In the barn."

I took off in a fume of fresh fears and suspicions.

Shirl, at least, hadn't killed her; this much was evident as I charged through the door. She was still on her feet, whickering and fretful as I—belatedly cautious—hauled up to consider each black lump of shadow in the roundabout threat of that heat-sticky dimness.

Stamping, impatient, she twisted her head to peer over a shoulder as, caught up in dark fancies, I continued to stare.

Daguerrias appeared. "I've kept the water away from her. She got her regular ration of everything last . . ."

I stepped over to look into her stall. "Did you put any straw—"

The horsemaster said in an offended tone, "How do you reckon I stayed on the circuit before I had you around to advise me?"

"Fetch her outside," I said, and headed for the yard.

She didn't give him any trouble, I noticed, when they came out. This close to a race most running stuff I'd seen would have been pretty rannicky. But though I went over her from teeth to tail I couldn't find any sign that she was ailing or had been tampered with. I made him move her around, even jump her over a stob. I still wasn't satisfied but "All right," I said, not able to think up any more tests. "Get those shoes off. When are you baiting her?"

"Well, anytime now." He was beginning to sound sullen.

"Have you walked her this morning?"

"You got me picked for a fool?" he said, looking ringy.

"Keep the water away and don't give her—"

"You know s' dang much suppose you take care of her!" Then he snarled, baring his teeth, "You can ride 'er, too!" and, flinging down her rope, went off in a huff.

I scooped up the halter shank, not as riled as you might guess. Matter of fact, I'd been intending to ride. Any disadvantage she'd be getting in weight and experience appeared a cheap exchange for a man I couldn't trust. I got off her shoes, put away the tools and, back in her box, gave her much less grain than she seemed to figure she had coming. Don't think horses can't express their minds. The look I got when no hay was forthcoming would have soured fresh cream.

When she was done I dampened a cloth, swabbed out her mouth and nostrils and, ignoring her displeasure, settled down outside her stall to while away what time we had left.

It was mid-afternoon when we appeared at Villalobos; Daguerrias, ponying Cajun Queen, up front in the lead where I could keep an eye on him. None of our tribe had elected to stay home, even Shirl crossed the river, which—in view of his diverse dark imaginings and what he had tried in the house with Linda—considerably astonished me.

He made a stiff black shape astride the heavy

muscled Granite, impervious to censure as the side of a mountain, dour and uncommunicative, jogging along with our two hired hands like Genghis Khan at the head of his bandits. His presence, boding no good whatever, turned me ever more restless and edgy, crammed as I was with my own stringent furies.

The air was oppressive. Weird with a strange, pervading lemon brilliance, the range stretched away bleak and lifeless as the moon. Nothing moved against the hills. The pink tower of the church stood stark as a sentinel above the motionless wilt of the trees. Every breath drew in the scorched smell of seared earth. What, I wondered, had become of Ybarra's herds—of the scrawny goddam cattle he had driven across the river?—the ones whose price we had mounted this race to determine.

Go on, you sonofabitch!—rain! I muttered to myself.

A man, if he is determined enough, can do just about anything. This was the rock to which I clung. If I had not been thoroughly convinced of this tenet I would not have bought those Waggoner horses or been sucked into this bastardly bind. That the whole situation was rapidly deteriorating was viciously apparent, yet I clung to my belief in man's determination, bound to the conviction that I was right and that dogged stubbornness could prevail. I couldn't let that girl come into my thinking.

Nothing, I swore, was going to stop Bancroft Benson—neither her nor that silly old popinjay Ybarra, nor anything Daguerrias and Shirl had cooked up. Not even, by God, those stupid papers I had signed.

As we rode into the plaza—Daguerrias still up front with Queen, then Shirl and his brush poppers and, finally, me—you could see some attempt had been made, in the Mexican manner, to brighten up this gala occasion with paper lantern strings and bits of colored bunting. Even Ybarra's peons, pouring out of mud huts like a scurry of mice, had got themselves up in their best hats and sashes to stand in barefoot grins and jabber as us crazy anglos, with our clubfooted mare, came like lambs for the shearing.

Don Alfredo, dazzling in braid and old-country velvets, clattered up with his daughter in an old coach-and-four still shabbily resplendent in crest and flaked paint and, in a muddle of out-riders armed with rusty *escopetas*, pulled up with a flourish reminiscent of trumpets.

The rickety vehicle groaned and screaked as he stood up in his magnificence to deliver his compliments. "Good friends," he declaimed, like a man selling snake oil, "I bid you fond welcome to the joys and hospitality of the Hacienda Villalobos—my house is yours." He bent his most lavish smile on me, spreading wide both arms. "After the *correr d prisa*—the race, we shall have the refreshments, the celebration and dancing. Let all be merry. My friends are yours." And, in his dark face, the teeth flashed again. Just like, I thought, the hungry grin of a crocodile—though this may have given him less than his due.

At least the "friends" trouping forward with their ladies and/or families from the direction of the casa seemed, if somewhat toplofty, to bear us no malice. Above slashed trousers and handsome jackets some of the faces, beneath those huge sombreros, reflected almost a kind of grudging admiration as though marveling at our brashness in bearding such a lion.

If this were so, it was not shared by the ragged mob of grinning and jabbering peons. Their convictions were as conspicuously apparent as the bell tower; they considered us loco and were making no bones of it.

The plane had been swept, in the native manner, with bundles of switches. As concession to the occasion, or in some pretense of civilized politeness, Ybarra's *vaqueros*—all fierce and skilled hombres—were here afoot, laughing and jostling with the brown-faced rest of that *paisano* rabble, their unwashed contaminations prudently contained behind a hedge of stretched *reatas*. Among the silver buckles and buttons and braid of the visiting *gente find* a few gem-studded weapons occasionally were visible, but beyond the ropes not even a *pistola* offended the proprieties ignored by Shirl and his two Texicans.

Above the tight-fitting waist of her butterfly dress Linda's dark eyes, all this while, had been on me, shyly filled with some message I would not read.

Now a barefooted boy, proud as Punch on Lágrimas, came out of the press, wildly cheered by the peons with shouts of *manífico*! and other, less distinguishable, tributes of their enthusiasm.

Ybarra, dismissing our animal with scarcely a glance, turned a strengthening frown in the direction of Daguerrias. "Is that fellow your rider?"

"With your permission, Don Alfredo, I will ride the mare myself."

"You, *señor*?" His brows shot up in evident astonishment. "The boy, Ysidro, will be upon Lágrimas . . ."

"That's all right."

He was not, apparently, the only startled hearer. There were more than a few peculiar stares. Daguerrias looked astounded and, the way Shirl stood straight up in his stirrups, a scorpion might have got up his pantsleg.

A little longer Ybarra eyed me. "Perhaps," he said, "we'd best be about it. I think we may be in for some rain."

I could not remember so awesome a sky. The

hills to the south were cut off like mesas by the high ridge of cloud blackly boiling across them.

Don Alfredo had beckoned up several *mozos*, was in the midst of issuing instructions, when I said, "You've likely noticed this mare is crippled. Besides the club foot, the walls of her hoofs are too thin to hold plates. We had to pull them."

"So?" Ybarra said.

"In view of these facts—and the additional handicap of a green rider weighing more than twice what your boy does—if it's all right with you we'd like to run on plowed ground."

He peered down his long nose, but I had spoken loud enough to reach most of his friends. The music arrived, three guitars and a brace of fiddles, one mouth harp and the grandfather of bass viols; and as the grinning faces stopped by the platform to await Don Alfredo's pleasure, he pawed his curly beard and, examining me with a somewhat more reticent appraisal, replied with a nod, "It shall be as you say."

He didn't have much choice the way I had put it, but I'd been ready if he'd balked to propose we ride owners; Don Alfredo weighed enough to offset any advantages he held.

"And where—?"

"That maize field will do," I said, pointing.

Shirl Dorrus pushed up with his face looking bony and the length of his scowl plainly shaped for trouble. But Ybarra, before he could pour out his spleen, gave rapid instructions in a crackle of Spanish. The men he had beckoned sprang away and the mustachioed driver, cramping his wheels, slammed the protesting coach in squealing clatter between where I was and Shirl's gurgling fury. The mob of *paisanos*, swarming over the ropes, broke in shouts for the maize, the *gente* in their wake and Bancroft Benson—never one to ignore opportunity's knock—departing with Queen after the boy on Lágrimas.

The ears, sun cured on their stalks, had not yet been harvested. I had thought to run between these stalks, but already a horde of willing brown hands was tearing the rattling growth out by the roots, clearing a swath that was three rows wide.

Don Alfredo, with his old man's love of pomp and tradition, would have saddled the affair with interminable adjustments had I not cried impatiently, "Let's get started. All we need's a couple of marks a quarter mile apart! Are we having a race or are we just going to stand around here discussing it?"

That brought his head around. He looked at me whitely, indignant and affronted, but waved his hand at two *mozos* toting sacks and told a third gruffly to leg off the distance. Then he looked at Queen again and, presently settling his ruffled feathers, apparently decided to overlook my lack of manners. What, after all, could one expect of a gringo?

I imagine, however, it was the mare that reassured him. With her uncurried hide, her tail filled with burrs, she stood on three legs looking half asleep. I could feel Linda's stare but kept my eyes on her father.

He peered thoughtfully about.

I said, "According to our agreement," and I was speaking to be heard, "we run this Texas fashion by the ask-and-answer method. The boy and me will take turns asking, and we don't cross the score until the asked one yells 'Go.' "

"But we might be here all night!" one of Ybarra's friends protested.

"I don't think we need worry about that," I said, looking around at the sky. The black boil of that cloud was much nearer and fiercer. "Well?" I said, looking again at Ybarra.

He'd gone back to studying Queen, face inscrutable. Compared to Lágrimas she looked like a cart horse, hipshot on my halter shank, head down, lip trembling. Short coupled and chunky her long underline was not pronounced in this posture. She didn't honestly look alert enough to catch a cold; and when, sighing mightily, she yawned, Ybarra nodded.

The *mozo* who had paced off the course waved a hand. The near line was drawn, brightly yellow, in cornmeal; and, from the legman's wave, apparently all was in readiness. A lot of the peons had gathered down there, and little huddles of them were stationed at various points along the way, grinning and jabbering, loudly offering wagers it seemed like no one would take. One of the group still around Don Alfredo wanted to know if I was permitted to ride without a saddle and the old man, shrugging, thoughtfully looked at me again.

"I'll put a surcingle on her," I said, and got down.

While I was busied with it Dorrus reappeared, forging through the press with more than usual insolence, coming up on Granite, his brace of bleach-eyed Texicans swarming after him like shadows, fanning out at either hand.

"How's it happen," he growled, looking hard at Ybarra, "I can't git up no bets here?"

Several of the *gente*, belatedly sauntering trackward, paused to twist their head and listen. I'll admit I was flustered, cold with shivers—but not Ybarra. If he was, he hid it well.

Linda, flushed and angry, surged erect, eyes blazing, but her father's dropped hand checked whatever brash thing she'd been minded to say. He spoke coolly enough. "I'll accommodate you."

"At what rate, old man?"

Ybarra's cheeks whitened. "Will ten to one be enough to amuse you?"

"That'll be just fine!" Shirl grinned at him nastily and, as the girl sank back, chucked a wad of rubber-banded currency in her lap. "There's five hundred smackers in that roll," he told Ybarra, "an' ever' damn dollar of it's on your hoss, Lágrimas!"

The old man, digesting this, looked stonily back and stiffly said nothing. The boy was too far away to have heard or be warned. The black stallion, curvetting under him, was becoming, impatiently, harder to control. Don Alfredo, looking his age, sat down rather shakily and motioned his coachman to get the rig rolling. They drove off, Ybarra's astounded friends hurrying after them.

I got onto the mare, but Shirl wasn't about to let me go without a warning. Before I could heel the mare into motion he got hold of her halter, grinning meanly around at me. "I been playin' your game, now you'll play mine. Make this look good, sport—but don't fergit," Dorrus said, "where my money's at."

With some mounts I've observed it was plain good looks, a particular skill, flashy way of going, some peculiar quirk individually their own or a downright lack of any suefulness at all, which most endeared a man to them and prompted highest praise.

You can judge for yourself how I felt about Queen. When I wheeled her away from Shirl and his jackals to come up with the boy down back of that line, it was hard to think why I'd chosen her over Granite. I couldn't turn up one likable quality. She had the same give and lurch you would have got from a busted spring.

In a way, of course, this simplified things. Shirl was fed up or he'd never have tried what he had yesterday. Tomorrow was shaping up for one hell of a squabble if this storm coming now did not cut off that banco. In a lot of ways, it looked like, the time had come to cut my losses and dig for the tules while I still had my health.

Lágrimas, when we finally got down there, was chafing so under the kid's tight hold, it seemed remarkably unlikely he could be held much longer. *He can't take much of that,* Shirl's man had said in proposing I insist on the Texas-fashion start. With the sweat that was on him from all this fiddling he looked fine drawn as a winter-starved cougar. The mare, head hanging, paid him no attention.

Suddenly, then, I got this notion. The coin I flipped gave the boy first answer. Hauling up the mare's head through a gobble of catcalls I whacked her across the butt with the halter shank. "Ready?" I called as we went lumbering lineward. But snorting, shaking his eye-rolling head, that crazy damned stud came crow-hopping sideways. We had to wheel and go back.

When we came up again you could see the kid was in trouble. That goddamn black had got the bit between his teeth. With his hands full of horse the boy gasped the question. Both of us abreast and pointed squarely at it, I suppose it seemed to the kid I had no choice but to agree. Anyway, he went.

You never heard such an uproar. One thing those *paisanos* could sure do was shout.

The sound of it turned ugly. A hundred yards out the kid looked back. You'd have swore those eyes of his got big around as slop pails. Through the bedlam of yells and cursing it took at least another fifty to get the stallion pulled up enough to risk coming round.

There were some hard things yelled, and a mort of angry faces, but I was in my rights and Don Alfredo knew it if nobody else did. Emulating the phlegmatic Queen I sat back for more comfort and twisted up a smoke.

Ybarra, standing up in his open-topped coach, was shouting and waving his arms for attention, but the racket got louder, the catcalls more vicious. They meant for me to know they wouldn't stand for that again.

The kid sidled by, standing up in his taps on the open-jawed, hard breathing, sweat soaked Lágrimas. To hell with his insults! Coming around on the mare I took a final deep drag and pitched my cigarette away. By now, I reckoned, we ought to be about even.

That boy sure looked ringy.

There wasn't going to be no more backing and filling. It was his turn to yell and I could see he would, regardless. He hauled the stallion around. I brought the mare about smartly and grabbed a handful of mane. It was my turn to ask but he knew I'd go this time and, as I'd suspected, wasn't waiting. While we were still ten feet this side of the cornmeal the little devil yelled *"Go!"* and hit the black with his reins.

I took hold with my knees and felt the mare flatten, like a cat sinking claws, just before we took off. If I hadn't had that neck hair to cling to I'd have been dumped sure. She tore away like we'd been shot from a cannon.

Ybarra's stallion had been launched from a running start and the kid, still ahead, was probably feeling pretty perky, but at about 220, warming into her drive, the Cajun Queen barreled past like that stud was standing still.

The kid, bent over, began swinging his rein ends.

Lágrimas, by his looks, was a half-mile horse. He was taller than Queen by a good full hand and, once the kid got him rolling—got him into his lick, he would likely pick up ground about as fast as we could leave it. Pretty soon, sure enough, I heard the *huh huh huh* of his deep-reaching breath.

He was coming up fast—no one had to tell me. Looking past the mare's ear I judged we'd come about 440—which left another eighth to go.

The black was lapped on us now. I could see his bared teeth, the red of flaring nostrils. From the corners of my eyes I saw that stretched black head creep forward, the kid crouched over his withers, still whaling.

I had to do something. I gave the mare her head.

Inch by inch we began to pull away. I held my breath, but her best was spent. I could feel the power dropping out of her. The sound of the black's pounding hoofs drew nearer, the *huh huh huh* of his lunging breath.

About a hundred yards off a blur of bug-eyed faces above a wall of shirts and cotton pantalones told me where the finish was. A hundred yards isn't anything at all in the mouth, but from the back of a hide that is coming apart that much stretched-out uncovered footage can look like forever.

I had on a pair of gut hooks but I was scared to throw them into her—even scratch or move my heels, lest the shift of weight put her off her stride. She was all heart and then some, giving everything she had, plumb willing to run the life right out of her, but the black's fire red nostrils was mighty near up to my knees again.

There was trembles all through her. She was wheezing now like a leaky bellows. You could tell she hadn't many more jumps left. It was neck meat or nothing! I drove in the spurs.

The weight of her head came off my arm. The next three jumps put the black back a foot. Above the search of the wind, above the thundering hoofs, I could hear the kid cursing. Hope began to pump into me. And then—don't ask me where, I saw the face of Shirl Dorrus!

Sixty . . . fifty . . . forty yards. The busted-spring lurch sent fresh shocks jolting through me; Lágrimas' nose was back at my knee. Gasp by gasp it crept to her withers, but still she hung on.

The kid began whaling at me with his rein ends and that way, still at it, we crossed the line with the mare's nose plainly in front by six inches.

I was in a vile mood as I led Queen back. The silence was unnerving, but no more frightening than the thoughts whirling through my head. Dorrus and me—as partners—were washed up and, because of him, all I had stood to gain in this country.

But to hell with that. What *really* gouged was the hateful remembrance of those missed chances with Linda. As Shirl had said bluntly, I could have married Villalobos.

The first drops of rain bit into the dust like silver dollars and this, I thought disgustedly, was probably the one that would do it.

Shoving through the last muddle of staring *paisanos* I cut over to the coach to deliver the mare and pick up the money we had coming for the cattle.

Ybarra was there. He had the sack and he was grinning. I supposed he had a right to feel good. Before either of us could get out a word Linda, running up, flung both arms around me.

I was not too stunned to take advantage of this good fortune. It was while I was reciprocating that Shirl, rounding the coach, wrenched the sack from her father and came for me with a leveled gun.

I pushed her away and jumped for him as flame tore out of its muzzle. Half blinded I crashed into him. That's all I've been able to remember. Don Alfredo told me later the Rurales had taken him, along with the hides they had cut off the cattle.

Center Point Large Print
600 Brooks Road / PO Box 1
Thorndike, ME 04986-0001 USA

(207) 568-3717

US & Canada:
1 800 929-9108
www.centerpointlargeprint.com